The Douglas Notebooks

The Douglas Notebooks

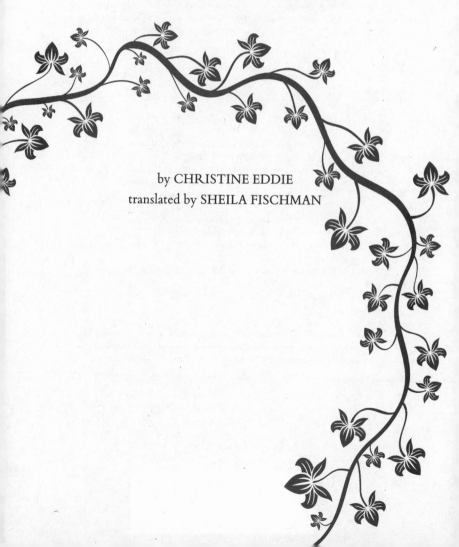

by CHRISTINE EDDIE
translated by SHEILA FISCHMAN

English translation copyright © 2013 by Sheila Fischman.
Original title: *Les carnets de Douglas*.
Copyright © 2007 by Christine Eddie.
Published in English under an arrangement with Les Éditions Alto.

Cover illustration: Veer.
Cover and book design by Julie Scriver.
Printed in Canada.
10 9 8 7 6 5 4 3 2 1

Library and Archives Canada Cataloguing in Publication
Eddie, Christine, 1954-
[Carnets de Douglas. English]
The Douglas notebooks / Christine Eddie; translated
from the French by Sheila Fischman.

Translation of: Les carnets de Douglas.
Issued also in electronic format.
ISBN 978-0-86492-619-7

I. Fischman, Sheila II. Title. III. Carnets de Douglas. English.

PS8559.D438C3713 2013   C843'.6   C2012-906318-5

Goose Lane Editions acknowledges the generous support of the Canada Council
for the Arts, the Government of Canada through the Canada Book Fund (CBF),
and the Government of New Brunswick through the Department of Tourism,
Heritage, and Culture.

Goose Lane Editions
500 Beaverbrook Court, Suite 330
Fredericton, New Brunswick
CANADA E3B 5X4
www.gooselane.com

I have in my heart a tree.

Christian Bobin
Mozart et la pluie

We exhaust ourselves travelling the earth, hunting for some treasure that will console. We hear the song of the sea. We read a poem. We inhale jasmine. We fall as the snow falls. We seek something dazzling that will reverberate again when the dull times return and punctuate the everyday, a meteoric brilliance that no human misery can crush.

I wanted to offer you the beauty of the world, a compendium of healing words that would guide you gently towards the light. That is all I have found to keep me from ever leaving you. It would have taken too long a time to understand that, here or elsewhere, away from you the light is always subdued. Some silences are unforgivable, and I try to reassure myself by thinking that at least I'll have spared you the spectacle of my collapse. But I'll write no more, this is my last notebook, I promise. I'm coming back. Wait for me.

Location

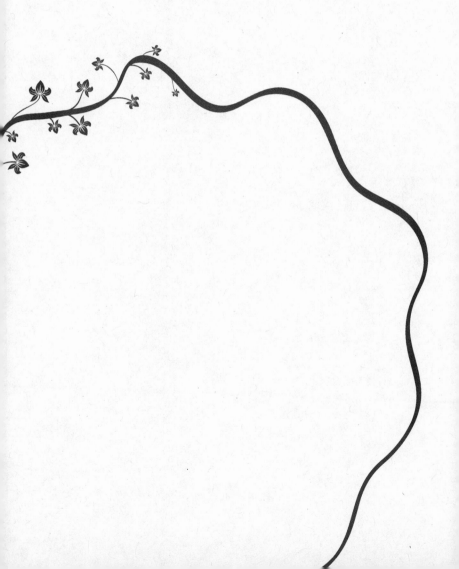

Even if fought far away, war is always profitable for someone. In Sainte-Palmyre, it was the Bradys. Guided by the smell of a fortune that was hidden at the slightest sign of rationing, they threw themselves into black market foodstuffs, the brewing of beer, and, above all, cooking up deals. Life went on, and before the ink that signed the Armistice was dry, their locomotive was already pulling a tidy fortune put together unbeknownst to the taxman.

Like a black tide, their power extended over dozens, then hundreds and thousands of hectares. Farms, slaughterhouses, grocery stores, factories, hotels: finally, people stopped counting. Everything that fed the region belonged to them in the end. In Sainte-Palmyre, the Bradys got in the habit of presiding over the table. First the father, then the son, that went without saying.

Antoine, offspring of the first generation of prosperous Bradys, guaranteed continuation as soon as he'd chosen a wife from among the daughters of prominent citizens: Alexina, a nymphet somewhat neurasthenic but with a substantial bank account. Their wealth secure, Antoine and Alexina had two children, a daughter, May, and—thank God!—a boy three years later. Which authorized the nymphet to sigh wearily when young Romain was introduced to illustrious visitors: "This will be my last child." She kept her promise.

Occupied—he making their assets bear fruit, she tending her depression—the Brady parents had little time to devote to Romain. As for May, the sister, her jealousy was transformed into aversion close to sadism whenever she had a chance to be alone with her brother. It happens.

Also, their younger son, though perfectly normal, never knew exactly how to behave with his nouveau riche family who kept up relations only if they were public. To the questions Romain asked—naively, timidly, like all children his age—they made no reply, or replied too quickly and off the point. Not now. How can you think such a thing? Will you please keep quiet! The little boy wandered the gleaming corridors of the manor house with its fake turrets; he hid in the folds of the curtains, hands stroking the heavy velvet; he curled up on the landing of the imitation marble stairs that was wide enough to hold two family trees. In the end, he did indeed keep quiet.

He could have got lost, shut himself away, but for the music that he heard by chance in the kindergarten, and the fact that Monsieur and Madame, thinking it would be polite now and then to offer their guests a recital, agreed to have him take lessons. Then there were the books imported for a small fortune, whole shelves at a time for the sake of appearance, whose pages were sometimes stuck together from never having been read. The real parents of Romain Brady, the only ones who truly mattered, were called Wolfgang Amadeus Mozart and the Comtesse de Ségur.

Living a four-hour drive from Sainte-Palmyre, Éléna Tavernier too had to be content with an empty childhood. She grew up in a house full of noise, in which the insults hurled by the father at the mother, Rose, along with a plate or a slap, were brimful of obscenity and contempt. Not to hear them demanded considerable effort from the little girl. She spent the better part of her early years with her ears blocked, dreaming that fairies would intervene and transport her and her maman to a land of wonders — any land at all. That was precisely what she'd been doing the last time her mother screamed in the kitchen while a spot of blood was growing into a lake on the floor. If a clue was needed to discover the whole truth, Éléna found it in the dead woman's terrified expression just before the priest closed her eyes. Denouncing the father, though, was beyond the strength of a child of six.

Rose Tavernier was buried at the end of the last row in Saint-Lupien's small graveyard, where Éléna could go only in secret, before school or after Mass, and she never had time to say Maman, I miss you. The only daughter had no choice but to put up with her only father. Like an invisible and peaceful chameleon, apparently obedient but in a constant state of alert, she learned how to tidy, clean, cook, and study while pretending not to be on guard at every moment. Chameleons, as is well known, have a visual field of three hundred and sixty degrees.

He's the baker's son, sighed Antoine Brady to the business-men passing through the parlour, astonished to see there a child deep in the adventures of Robinson Crusoe. He's my adoptive brother, May hastened to add to her giggling friends on Sunday, as if to apologize for having to impose on them the scales and arpeggios that were taking over the three floors of the manor. . . . The last child I'll have, mumbled Alexina, wrapping herself in her cashmere shawl.

Romain couldn't stand up straight. Romain waddled like a duck. Romain put his elbows on the table and, more often than not, started fights. Romain was too much this and not enough that. When a word dared to exit his mouth, it disconcerted. It wearied his mother, irritated his father. Awkwardness, foolishness, absent-mindedness. All was Romain's fault. Even the rain that rotted the crops.

"You've got the evil eye," May grumbled into his ear, sinking her nails into the flesh of his arm.

He did his best to mature, though, by searching for a hidden meaning behind the facts of life. Still, at school, the baker's son took his place in the middle of the pack, from where he did nothing to draw attention to himself. In company, the adopted son didn't try to make friends but let himself become the laughingstock of the inha-bitants of Sainte-Palmyre, whom he observed without flinching. Very early, however, Alexina's last child made a decision that he had plenty of time to ripen before he fell asleep at night, counting the pocket money he was saving.

During the ostentatious ceremony held in honour of his eighteenth birthday, to which were invited handfuls of strangers, Romain surprised his parents by announcing that he was leaving to live in the country for a while. His sister burst out laughing.

On the morning she would leave Saint-Lupien, Éléna wakened suddenly in an empty house. As often happened, her father hadn't come home. She took advantage of his absence to set out for school before dawn. Along the way she would stop at the graveyard, where she would place a bouquet of wild violets at the end of the last row.

Standing in front of her dead mother, her school bag in one hand and the barely open blue flowers in the other, the girl tried to recall a memory that would evoke something gentle and strong from a far-off time when life for the two of them still contained — if her father did them the favour of slipping away — an afterthought of affection. But aside from the fine mist that was dancing on the poorly maintained grass along the paths, nothing showed up.

The poor-quality tombstone looked at her sadly as the sun rose. The letters that formed her mother's name were erased in places, already darkened by time and the elements. When the birds launched into their loud cheeping to greet the dawn, Éléna, who was staring at her mother, could no longer read Rose Tavernier, only *ose Ta v . . . ie. Ose ta vie*. Dare to live.

She stayed there, motionless and taken by surprise. A wild urge to step out of line ran through the veins of the chameleon.

Neither his parents nor his sister nor his clarinet teacher had believed Romain.

"And who do you think will provide for your needs?" they mocked.

"We'll see," replied Romain, avoiding their skeptical looks.

There was certainly a little discussion, but just for form's sake. Because, at the end of the day, the fact that their son had a sudden urge to treat himself to a few weeks in a field was a relief to the Bradys, who felt that some distance between them, even brief, would be beneficial to the whole family. They greeted the news with chuckles, sure that, in any case, as soon as he was confronted with the rigours of rural life, their son and heir would come running home.

When the snow had melted completely, young Romain stuffed his gear into a bag to which he added a compass, an axe, a package of seeds, and some matches. With the bag at his feet and the clarinet case in his hand, he said a cool goodbye to his mother, his sister, and the servants, as he'd been taught, bowing slightly.

Antoine Brady, never there at crucial moments, had shut himself away in his office, where he broke into a grin that had no witnesses. Focusing vaguely on a column of figures, glad that his inept son was making a decision and sticking to it, he was smiling. Upstairs, watching the scene from a window, the music teacher was smiling even though he was worried, for the Bradys were his most significant source of income and Romain his best pupil by far. Standing on the threshold of the manor, Alexina was smiling too, enchanted by the unusual nature of the event, while May was rejoicing to see her fondest dream come true. Even the domestics were smiling, pleased to have one less room to tidy. Life was smiling on Romain Brady, who had fear glued to his stomach. When it was time, he picked up his travelling bag and started walking. He did not turn around.

In Saint-Lupien, Éléna was getting ready to do the supper dishes when out of the blue her father announced that he'd promised her to the grocer's son in exchange for a case of Scotch. Éléna would have slit her wrists rather than marry, so young, such a big lump of a man who could neither laugh nor read. Which was what she replied, but her father retorted that he had no intention of asking her opinion and ordered her to shut her goddamn trap.

Belches interrupted the father's grunting. Staggering towards Éléna, he raised an arm to hit her and began to spit insults. The girl ran to the front door. Along the way, she grabbed the first thing that came to hand, an oil lamp that shed a harsh light on the room, and hurled it impulsively at the fuming hulk. She opened the door to rush into the night, unaware of the fire that was already sweeping through the dilapidated house.

It was not until she hadn't enough breath to keep going, on the other side of the cornfield with its dry, winter-blackened stalks, that Éléna collapsed. She was cold and could no longer feel her scraped ankles. Her heart was pounding so hard that she felt as if she were being pursued by an army of soldiers. It took her another few minutes to realize that she was out of danger. Getting a grip on herself, she resumed her race, determined to get as far away as possible from the deserted plain where she had always lived. In the distance, a house was burning. One might have said that the sun, for the second time that day, was coming up.

In Sainte-Palmyre, the harvest season was going full tilt and Antoine Brady was kept busy calculating the profits, gross and net, from his truck farming. The time had come to choose a college for Romain, and Madame his mother had finally started studying what various private establishments had to offer — all of them prepared to bow and scrape to welcome a Brady among their donors. As for May, she was counting the hours between the beauty parlour and a tennis champion who was introducing her to the delights of lengthy kisses.

In the afternoon, there was dramatic pressure on the stock market and Monsieur double-locked himself inside his office. Alexina dragged out a telephone call to a school principal who was explaining the attractions of a novel method for teaching quantum physics, grovelling all the while. May, meanwhile, was wriggling on the tennis court, her weight on her right leg, both hands clutching the racquet, gaze focused on her opponent's biceps, not his ball. The servants, who needed instructions to prepare for Harvest Day, an annual feast to underline with pomp the fame of the Bradys of Sainte-Palmyre, demanded Romain, for want of anything better. Which forced the others to face facts: the son hadn't come home. Honestly, that child!

Other investigations had to be launched. Nearly a month went by before anyone noticed that something serious might have happened. The searches ended on All Saints' Day, when Antoine Brady allowed his advisers to convince him that pursuing their efforts was unrealistic. On Christmas Eve, policemen showed up at the manor and stared at the floor as they told the family that a decomposed body found next to a stream a few kilometres from a nearby town was without a doubt that of Romain. They were sorry.

The following week, a short private ceremony was held to commemorate the dead man's brief existence.

Romain Brady had walked north for seventy-six days before he found a forest vast and deep enough for stopping. He had disappeared into it to look for a river. He paced his territory several times before deciding on the spot where he would settle.

Building a den was no easy task. The first winter, though not particularly harsh, left Romain with a fever because of the wind and snow that seeped inside through the cracks in the unhewn timber. When the days began to grow shorter again, though, Romain knew that he would never again fear the cold so much. His cabin built of superimposed logs may not have been very big, but the fireplace of large grey stones would keep it warm. The thickness of the walls, cemented with a mixture of grass and mud, would keep him cool in summer. Carefully corded wood was waiting in the lean-to.

Romain was thinner and exhausted, but content. A number of villages were at most a day's walk away, and he soon realized that he would not lack any essentials. The river provided clear water and abundant pike and trout. The earth in the clearing grew the seeds that he'd taken over the weeks from big vegetable gardens in Sainte-Palmyre. The forest was home to game. The sun dried clothing. Snow, salt, and the cool water in the streams preserved food.

Pocket money was useful for obtaining essential foodstuffs, as well as materials that couldn't be found in the woods. Glass for the opening in the wall on the south side. Candles and sugar. An aluminum pan for collecting rainwater. A flexible tube that completed an ingenious water supply system. And whenever one miraculously appeared, a book.

Each day devoted to making new acquisitions was an exacting adventure. He had to travel a long road, not arouse the suspicions of the locals regarding the young man who didn't say much but always paid on the spot, with fresh fish or small banknotes, clean and smooth, that he took slowly out of the pocket of an already well-worn parka. Admittedly, Romain Brady's intermittent presence in the vicinity made tongues wag. But so many young people were wandering then, in search of a new life, that Romain managed to be relatively anonymous. A reassuring and familiar state that suited him now more than ever.

Despite the warm welcome by the Little Sisters of Saint Carmel when she knocked on their door, Éléna had no intention of staying in the convent very long. She did enjoy singing the psalm of the day with them while peeling vegetables, but she definitely didn't like the silence in the refectory, and she never heard a call to the contemplative life amid the clink of soup spoons. If the cloistered nuns had known that their favourite wasn't even sixteen yet, they no doubt wouldn't have let her leave. But given the lovely child's determination and self-confidence, they weighed her down with food, clothes, and way too much advice.

In Éléna's cardboard suitcase, lovingly filled by the multitude of her new mothers, was the address of a cousin of the old nun who did the bookkeeping. The cousin's name was Mercedes, she was an apothecary, and she lived in Rivière-aux-Oies. The prudent nuns started a novena so that Éléna would be able to find it, because the place was a mere comma, too discreet to appear on a map. Even the trail that went there could be hard to follow, because of the incredible zigzags in the bits of road stuck together in the vicinity, none of which went precisely to the village.

Éléna rode the bus and took advantage of the few cars that climbed up there before arriving safe and sound. Holding the nuns' letter, she went into what seemed to be the only store around and asked shyly if anyone knew

Mercedes. Fifteen minutes later, she met a small, squat, energetic woman who greeted her noisily, gave her food and lodging, and, before a week had passed, suggested that the girl become her apprentice. You'll take over from me, you'll have a trade. Éléna, who in truth had no alternative, didn't need coaxing. And so, alongside the pharmacist, she made every effort to learn the names of plants, their miraculous effects on rheumatism, headache, and melancholy. Unassuming, she learned how to make compounds with strange aromas that were placed as a poultice on the site of the pain; potions; tincture of hawthorn; unguents of citronella; and powders made from seeds whose names could be found in a big illustrated book that she studied zealously.

People sometimes came from far away to ask Mercedes for advice. In the end, they trusted her assistant as well. A rumour was already spreading beyond the immediate area: the witch in Rivière-aux-Oies had found a magician.

After his second winter in the woods, loneliness fell onto Romain like a bear on a butterfly. The snow had melted in rivulets around the cabin and the earth was beginning to dry. Buds were peacefully dressing the forest, creating a green mist on the tops of the leafy trees. The sun was playing there as if sun and trees hadn't known each other for 380 million years. A family of deer was grazing calmly on the ground rich with summer, though in this season it offered only a brownish mulch. Raccoons were emerging from their dens, strolling awkwardly, and birds in a windless sky were chirping, each one louder than the other. Even the shriek of the squirrels, so irritating on some days, evoked a semblance of happiness.

So much beauty stirred a profound sorrow in Romain. The wood was cut and the water tank filled to the brim. In what he liked to call his workshop but was in fact simply an archway made of a rudimentary assemblage of branches, a second chair awaited some touch-ups before finding its place in the cabin. It hadn't occurred to Romain that it would likely never be of any use to him. Noting bitterly that, after the excitement of the survival measures, he now must be content with living, he listened for a moment to the lilting tangle of nature and sought a comrade in the lively crowd surrounding him. But the animals, accustomed to his presence, paid no attention to him.

He had not yet dared take out his clarinet lest the sound of the instrument betray his presence. On that day he pulled it feverishly from its case, screwed it together, and adjusted the reed. From the moment he attuned his breathing and his fingers, music lifted him off the ground. Standing in Mozart's hot-air balloon, holding the composer by the neck, Romain felt his soul become lighter than a maple key.

From walking along the clump of trees in search of
chanterelles or white elderberries, Éléna had domesticated
the area surrounding the forest and walked a little more
deeply into it each time. She felt nearly at home until, of
course, what would happen, happened.

Early on, she'd had a hunch that the forest at Rivière-
aux-Oies was inhabited. Although Mercedes had told her
that the white man had chased away all those who used to
live in the territory, the young girl didn't believe a word.
Certain clues are unmistakable: too-recent paths, entire
clumps of blueberries stripped of their fruit, plants
trampled by something heavier than a hare or a fox in
the spring. Éléna was well aware that she was not alone
in being enamoured of the forest. Excited by the call of
adventure, she didn't breathe a word, especially not to
Mercedes.

At all times, but maybe especially in the spring, the
tamaracks stretched out with surprising charm. One day,
when she was advancing farther than usual towards one of
them, Éléna thought she heard the strange and desperate
cry of a chorus of mourning doves, but — in the middle
of the woods? Or was it the lapping of the river, whose
winding course she had not yet been able to locate. Or just
the wind, pinned inside a heap of dried leaves? The wind
sometimes makes the strangest sounds.

Eyes peeled, she slowed down before stopping a
hundred metres from a clearing. Even the birds had

fallen silent. What they were listening to sounded like
a revelation, luminous and light. The space was wrapped
in ecstasy and disenchantment together. Éléna's closed eyes
misted over despite herself. It lasted an eternity, around
seven minutes. She was making the acquaintance of an
adagio for clarinet, and dumbfounded, she discovered
a heap of points in common with it.

"I think you go to the woods a lot."

Mercedes noticed a change in her pupil, but the normally chatty girl refused to confide in her. New spring plants, a sudden need for solitude, a nest to protect, an injured wren — the pretexts differed every time Mercedes tried to find something out. Though disappointed, the old woman stopped insisting and soon had no influence over the comings and goings of Éléna, who took off, apparently, as soon as she was out of bed.

And so, nearly every day, Éléna hopped onto Mercedes' rusty bicycle and belted down the road, hiding the bike under a clump of Juneberry trees, and plunged into the forest of Rivière-aux-Oies. Accustomed to the route, she took one path and then another, turning left then right, skirted the stump of a tremendous balsam fir, then went left again. Spying on the big wild man was a full-time occupation.

Romain seemed to suspect nothing. Up early, he had already cut wood, hoed the vegetable garden, checked his snares. Éléna found him at work on his bark canoe (so big, she thought, it would take him years to finish), making a snare, or simply sitting on a log reading, eating, or thinking. Hidden far away behind a copse of black spruce, she waited patiently. Listening to the big wild man play his small instrument had become Éléna's reason for living.

One day, she didn't find him.

Romain had left at dawn with carefully wrapped fresh fish and rabbit skins in his bag. He would trade them for flour and new tools. He would go to the barber as well, because even without a mirror he could tell that his unkempt hair and scruffy beard needed work.

He walked on the side of the road and hopped into a passing truck for a lift to one of the nearest villages. Like all outsiders Romain met since leaving his old life, the driver had bombarded him with indiscreet questions, around which the young man now skated deftly. His ready-made answers recounted in a perfectly plausible way that he was a biologist who'd left the big city (that was enough to justify his eccentric appearance) to cross the country and perfect his observation of the migratory routes of certain bird species. Starting there, what Romain had to say was crammed with dull scientific details that generally brought the conversation around to more impersonal topics: the weather, the terrible state of the roads, the indifference of the government...

"Ah! So you're Mr. Starling?"

"Starling?" (Why not? Romain thinks.)

"Sure, the bird that adapts to everything and talks all the time! When I saw you, I thought, Now there's a weird bird."

While the trucker-ornithologist was still chortling, the young man hastened to get off at the next crossroads. He walked a while longer before arriving in the village.

He ate in a tavern. The fries were limp and greasy. At the market, he had to haggle for a long time before he could trade his trout and his skins. The people in this village were suspicious, he couldn't get over it. Still, he found a nearly new copy of the poems of Alain Grandbois, which filled him with joy. He almost forgot the barber and did not set out for home until much later, taking long strides.

Sunk in thought, Romain was surprised by the storm. Night was beginning to fall and you couldn't see much. Soaking wet, head down, he was chewing up the kilometres at a good steady pace when he thought he spied a white shape charging towards him on a bicycle. He tried to throw himself into the ditch but only had time to feel a pain that broke his body in two. Then, nothing.

A heavy rain was falling onto the dirt road that ran along the forest at Rivière-aux-Oies. Éléna and Romain opened their eyes at the same time, each as scared as the other. He tried to get up. His broken ribs slowed him down and made him wince. She was up long before him, mud all over her face and clothing, scratches on her legs and arms that didn't hurt now. Very agitated, she didn't stop talking but didn't make sense. So much so that Romain, horrified, thought for a moment that he was back in Sainte-Palmyre, putting up with his sister's unbearable chatter.

When it skidded, the bike had lost a wheel, which Éléna was frenetically looking for in the growing dark. When she found it, she wanted to put it back on right away. Romain was finally, painfully, standing up. He looked at the thin girl, dripping wet, who did not even apologize for trying to kill him. Seeing her panicking over the twisted mudguard, he rummaged slowly in his bag and took out a pair of pliers. He held them out to her. She hardly seemed surprised that he had on him the exact tool she needed.

"Breathing hurts," he managed to say.

"Yes," she said, not understanding. "Sometimes it hurts to live."

They were silent, and for a quarter of an hour Éléna seemed concerned only about her bicycle. Once her fear had passed and she was sure that she could get back to Mercedes' place safe and sound, she took the time to realize that the beardless, silent youth she'd run down might be the big wild man. She didn't let her distress show, and as soon as she was able to leave she returned the pliers, giving him a brief look of gratitude. At least, that was how Romain interpreted Éléna's frightened half smile before she turned and went on her way.

The white shape disappeared as quickly as it had arrived, and it was another hour before Romain arrived at the door of his cabin.

It rained for six days in a row. Éléna spent them shut away in her bedroom, sick with a bad flu and taciturn again.

Mercedes, too worried to be angry, had greeted her without making a fuss. She had phoned Dr. Patenaude. (Maliciously, behind his back, they called him Pressing Cloth, a reference to the countless handkerchiefs, always clean and ironed, that he'd take from his pocket and politely offer the ladies.) The doctor had arrived out of breath, reassuring. Plenty of rest, plenty of heat. He trusted completely the apothecary's wisdom, and he'd insisted at length that she mustn't hesitate to call him if the fever persisted.

It wasn't necessary. Waiting on the young girl hand and foot, Mercedes could see her state improving. She would knock on her door and, even if she didn't get an answer, go in with a bowl of hot soup, freshly baked bread, and a tisane of mallow. Bending over the sulky girl's bed, the old woman would tuck her in and spend hours at her side.

"I told you not to go wandering. You have to learn to obey, Éléna. You're too young to do just as you like. Éléna, are you listening?"

Not a word. Scarcely a grunt.

One morning, when she was tidying up around the bed without making a sound because the patient was still asleep, Mercedes spied the leather handle of the clarinet case sticking out from under the mountain of pillows. Pulling the object away so that Éléna wouldn't hurt herself while she slept, she decided it was time they had a talk.

It rained for six days in a row and Romain spent them on his back in his damp shelter. Alone and unwell, he thought he would die there in the middle of the forest at Rivière-aux-Oies. He was starting to breathe more easily, but unable to move normally, he lived on just water and berries. He remained shut away. The bit of strength he had left was used for brooding. Which was all he did — brood and sleep. Between brief moments of drowsiness, he experienced again, like a nightmare, the incident with the cyclist. He kept turning over and over the phrase she'd dropped negligently, as if the words did not carry a contagious grief. *Sometimes it hurts to live.* What did she know about it? Romain would grow agitated, gazing at the framework of the roof. It can happen that we no longer know where the day begins and where it ends. That living is unbearable. And diabolical? Was she familiar with the diabolical, Ms. Public Menace?

He did not hear Éléna knock and started when the door opened, reviving the pain in his injured ribs. She had dirty shoes, a bag that seemed heavy, and eyes that were trying to get used to the dimness. He didn't recognize her right away.

"Anyone home?"

Once the shock was over, he muttered an uninviting sound. She didn't seem to take offence. She had brought food and she'd come for news. Introducing herself, she set down her bag, took off her anorak, shook it, and tossed it on the table. She pulled a chair over to the bed and undid a damp scarf that was holding back her long, black, curly hair that he hadn't noticed the first time. She was still as thin and voluble (but less strange, thought Romain). Her exuberance created a diversion. As did the peanut butter cookies. He decided not to throw her out right away.

They didn't hear the rain stop. They didn't see the rainbow circle the forest.

At first, Éléna's presence affected Romain like a monstrous and ill-mannered intrusion. His physical distress, however, did not allow him to quibble about the kind of help that Providence had finally decided to send him. The cyclist insisted on coming back. He began by making sure that she wouldn't ask any questions and that she would be discreet (he made her swear), then muttered something that the girl interpreted favourably. Eventually he would get used to her visits, and even if admitting it was out of the question, he ended up looking forward to them.

Éléna, for her part, first went to the heart of the forest in Rivière-aux-Oies prompted by a powerful feeling of guilt. What was most urgent was to return the magical object from which she could draw only false notes when she'd tried to explain to Mercedes that it was a treasure with extraordinary properties. She was able, the first time she came by, to put the case away in the exact same place where she'd found it in the empty cabin a week before. Afterwards, she persisted in seeing the injured man with the hope, weak but constant, that he would consider thanking her with new recitals. The more Romain put off expressing anything like gratitude, the more frenetically she pedalled towards the woods.

Romain's condition was improving. Éléna had made a soft bandage in which she'd inserted some skunk cabbage leaves that soothed the pain and that she insisted on changing herself, which terrified the convalescent.

It created between them a kind of intimacy filled with modesty, all the more mischievous because the cabbage earned its name well. But little by little, Romain's movements regained their ease and an awkward gaiety finally took hold of him.

We often imagine that love must gush forth spontaneously, surround itself with disarming turmoil, and
blossom with a roar. Yet love also advances with muffled
tread.

First, there were the lies to unravel. Romain Brady
wasn't called Just Plain Starling, as he had told Éléna
the first time she entered his place. He wasn't a biologist,
and he had never travelled the country in search of the
red-eyed towhee, of which he'd heard say that some were
now nesting north of Cape Cod.

Éléna had not found Romain's shelter by following his
tracks on the muddy paths. She was not discovering the
kingdom and the customs of the big wild man she'd been
observing for weeks. Nor did she keep the secret, because
in the evening, when she went back to Mercedes' place,
she told the whole story. Well, almost the whole story.

Romain had no experience of trust and he hadn't the
slightest idea of the road to take to find it. Éléna, for her
part, obsessed by the clarinet still shut away in its case
and stashed behind the wood next to the fireplace, was
beginning to despair of ever hearing it again.

Unravelling the lies took a very long time.

Before he was healed, Romain had to learn to talk. His habit of silence and suspicion still kept him paralyzed. While Éléna was bursting with spontaneity, he stumbled over words, didn't complete his sentences, changed the subject at the drop of a hat, and awkwardly used onomatopoeia too much. Days passed before they talked informally, then a shared smile established the possibility of a confidence.

They were sitting on some big warm rocks alongside the river. Éléna told the story of Rose Tavernier. In a single breath, she wanted to introduce her mother to Romain, show him a face, eyes, and hands that she invented on the spot because children's memory is perishable, invent for her a life that wouldn't have been frittered away on the deserted plain of Saint-Lupien, but on the contrary would be spread out with panache, recalling the beauty of Rose Tavernier when she put on her little veiled hat to go to Mass, the grace of her laugh, a laugh so rare that it embodied the very idea of happiness for a six-year-old little girl. A Rose Tavernier larger than life, brave and loving, who pushed her daughter in the old tire made into a swing that Rose herself had hung up on the only tree next to the house, a Rose who made pancakes with molasses on Saturday mornings and encouraged Éléna to learn how to read, who dreamed of a life for her a hundred times more appealing than that in Saint-Lupien. A Rose Tavernier who would not be dead at twenty-four, her head shattered against the yellow wall of the kitchen, the blood from her brain forming a lake on the floor.

"*Ose ta vie*. Dare to live," Éléna murmured when she'd finished.

Romain had listened without budging. He laid his hand lightly on Éléna's shoulder, now more and more aware that, with his forefinger, he could lightly touch her black curls. They stayed that way, side by side, amid the growl of the torrent and the same old story sung by the wind in the aspens.

There was so much sunshine that summer that the tomatoes in the garden threatened to die long before they were ripe. Romain and Éléna devoted days at a time to rescuing tomatoes and to walks through the trees, where they inventoried species and picked mushrooms and swam in the river, whose flow, slowed down by a drop in the water level, made them think they could swim.

Éléna revealed the mysteries of plants to Romain. She taught him that red foxes are born blind and deaf. She told him the strange legend that had given Rivière-aux-Oies its name, and how the Natives used porcupine quills to decorate their utensils or moose hide for making snowshoes.

Romain taught Éléna to tell the difference between the crow's croak and the raven's caw. He explained that young birds lay smaller eggs than their elders, that twenty-five thousand species of insects live in the forest, that it's necessary to protect the peregrine falcon and to wait patiently for the magnificent spectacle of the return of the snow geese.

But Romain's favourite sphere was that of trees. He could identify their species, notch them to extract their sap, and choose with care those that could be felled without disturbing their neighbours. He knew the history of every one, knew that the black spruce lives only in North America, that the great white pine had disappeared a half-century earlier, and that the grey squirrel is incredibly good at reforesting because it forgets where it has hidden seeds.

A ritual settled in. In the late afternoon, before they parted, Romain described to Éléna the hundreds of trees whose names rang out like a trip around the world. The Australian monkey puzzle tree, the African star chestnut, the nettle tree of Provence, the cedar of Lebanon, the Himalayan juniper, the Szechuan poplar. Never, though, did he dare talk to her about the Mediterranean Judas tree, which is also known as the love tree.

By the hottest part of the summer, Romain was fully healed, but he still hadn't played the clarinet in front of Éléna, or even recalled the role that music played in his life. After much dithering that she thought was clever but that fell flat, she decided to make the first move.

They were picking raspberries, waving away the mosquitoes while they compared harvests, laughing.

"How long have we known each other, Starling?"

"I don't know, Éléna.... Three months?"

"And when do you intend to say something about yourself?"

Seeing him close himself away, she tried to make up for it, slammed down her bucket so quickly that she nearly knocked it over. She approached him. Romain was as strong as she was frail, and he had a good smell of beard and muscles. She whispered in his ear an apology for her hasty behaviour, but when their faces touched again, she impulsively moved her mouth towards his.

"No," he said, stepping back.

"Why?"

She faced him, stoic. She waited. He said nothing, but he'd turned pale. Then, in a voice barely audible:

"You don't know me. I...I can make the harvest rot."

It was a start. She took his hand.

That night, Romain talked as long as there were stars in the sky, and when the moon changed continents, they'd already shared most of their secrets. Then Elena suggested that Romain choose what he wanted her to call him from now on. The exercise quickly became a game, and they played for a moment, making up some extravagant names.

"Tragopogon?"

"Harmattan, like the wind?"

"No, Styrax! Styrax like the perfume tree...."

Romain quite liked Styrax. But as seriously as she could, and looking him straight in the eye, Éléna told him that she wanted to give him the name of the tallest, sturdiest, most spectacular of trees. And thus was born Douglas Starling, whose first act was to get up and search behind the corded woodpile next to the fireplace. Éléna thought her chest would explode: at last, Mozart came into her life to stay.

Close-Up
(and fade to white)

Ah yes, love can be grandiose.

For Douglas, Éléna chose the body that best suited her. She asked the humidity to curl her hair even more, asked the sun to colour her cheeks. The river water softened her skin and the light brightened her eyes. She pulled on her Sunday legs and dressed in her prettiest breasts. She held on to her good humour and her laugh began to reverberate in the forest. Loving Douglas made her happier.

For Éléna, Douglas unlocked his heart. Shyly at first, then with confidence, like a window opening slowly onto the sea. In her presence he emptied old drawers, letting his fears fly away one by one, freed from the torment where he'd kept them closed up. He dusted off his loneliness. With the help of Mozart, Liszt, Schumann, and Debussy, he gave her the gift of tenderness stamped with grace. And between the yellowed pages of his poetry books, he found the words of love. Loving Éléna made Douglas more human.

When I was a child, Éléna confided, and still going to the country school in Saint-Lupien, Madame Taillon, the teacher, wanted me to talk about life with my father. I knew that, because Madame Taillon would settle her big, nervous schoolteacher's eyes on me while her right hand kept taking off and putting on her glasses, and she said things to me that I never heard her say to anyone else. Was there something I'd like to confide to her? Had I had enough to eat? Slept? That bruise on my arm? Was it?

I had got to the point of dreading Madame Taillon's cross-examinations more than anything. Because if she kept it up, I would dissolve in tears and let myself be taken away by the teacher and maybe by the chief of police. They would put me in an orphanage, where I'd have to stay till I turned eighteen. So one day, I told her: Don't worry, Madame Taillon, I love my father more than myself, and our house smells of lilacs and pea soup.

I knew that the aroma of lilacs and pea soup would keep the teacher and the chief of police calm. I knew that lying as a way out is easier than it seems, and that, using it, I could always put off until later all sorts of trouble. From the day I met you, though, I've stopped cheating.

"Are you sure?"

"I swear on my mother's grave."

When I was a child, Douglas confided, I was already so tall that no arm was long enough to hug me and I was so tedious that only the clouds and the trees would listen to me and I oozed so much trouble that, even on Christmas Day, my mother cried and my father thought that the world was on the road to ruin because there was nothing to be done with the boy. You wouldn't have liked me when I was little.

"I'd have liked you even if you were an earthquake," said Éléna.

The forest cast a spell over them. When they opened the door in the morning, they would take a few steps in the clearing, examining the vegetable garden, and enter a theatre devoted to beauty, inhabited by a crowd of giants that opened up towards the light.

There were those that stayed with them all winter, clad from head to toe in branches laden with needles and cones where half the birds in the country were hidden. Spruce trees, a little scrawny but standing together in large clumps. Fir trees with greyish trunks swollen with blobs of resin. Some pine trees with a haughty bearing.

Then there were the others, touching with their foliage that showed better than the sky where they were on the calendar. Douglas reckoned that some were at least two hundred years old. Birches, willows, aspens, some maples, more rarely a red oak. They shivered in the slightest breeze, and listening to them made one a poet.

Éléna's gaze, though, was always focused farther away, as far as the tamaracks that stood out in the background like merry acrobats. Neither broad-leafed nor conifers, they formed a separate group, a somewhat crazy orchestra in the midst of sensible and careful musicians. When Douglas and Éléna opened the door in the morning, those were the ones they greeted first.

"And if you became a stream?"

"I would want you to be thirsty."

"And the air? If you were the air?"

"Mmmm... I would want you to know how to breathe."

"Yes, but if..."

He was like that, Douglas, when he was Éléna's lover. He mended her soul with unexpected words full of honey, and finally she forgot once and for all her old rancour towards Saint-Lupien. He had his own way, kind and attentive, of making her believe in everything she wanted to believe in. Even at night, when the forest became intimidating and was covered with black darkness.

"You're my rudder. Stay with me, Curly Girl."

My rudder, my compass, my lightning rod. That was him, all right. Not to have spoken for twenty years, then suddenly knowing a whole dictionary of love words. To adorn her with expressions full to the brim. To raise her up with a phrase, settle her at the peak of rapture, and do nothing to bring her back down. To name her as one baptizes a world long coveted, now conquered at last. He couldn't help it. Because the sun spattered her face. Especially at night.

Happiness spent one whole year with them, a year during which they travelled back and forth between the forest and the village of Rivière-aux-Oies. Éléna, loyal to Mercedes, continued to assist her. Meanwhile, Douglas would go hunting for the treasure that would fix his problem of the moment—nails, rope, a piece of metal...Often the two of them would set off on the old bike, until one day its chain gave up on them, leaving them grinning on the side of the road where they learned to walk hand in hand, telling one another their little stories. In winter they put on snowshoes, and in February they had to spend one whole night outside, huddled under a makeshift shelter, until the blizzard had passed. In the spring, they were absolute masters of an estate whose every hiding place they knew.

At the end of another summer, they had enough wood and blankets, preserves and jars of jam, salt fish and water to last from freeze-up to spring when the river thawed. Éléna knew how to make bread, clothes, and medicines. Douglas could transform a stump into whatever they needed. He had spent days sealing the canoe with a patch made of melted fir resin mixed with animal fat. Then he set to work in the cabin until it finally looked like a house. A second window, a better-insulated floor, a bigger bed, a flower box to make Éléna happy...

Through the new window, unbeknownst to him, she watched him stroke the trees. She listened to him talk to

them before he lopped them. She observed how carefully
he fortified the regrowth, assessed the condition of the
foliage; she also observed the reverence he bestowed on
the slightest young shoot. Éléna was moved, and ran to
fetch some birch bark to write to Douglas what she didn't
know how to say in person. She leaned against the oldest
of the tamaracks, her face bent forward, fully absorbed in
her prose. He acted as if he hadn't noticed anything, busy
slowly planing the floor plates of the canoe that were
already smooth enough, and he devoured her with
his eyes, ready to turn away suddenly if she decided to
raise her curly head towards him. I was alone, thought
Douglas, and now I am unique. How had such a miracle
happened? Éléna stopped writing for a moment to
examine more closely an insect hidden under a dead
leaf. All at once, he dreamed of being a beetle.

Annoyed, Mercedes became annoying when she scolded Éléna energetically for the growing gap between them. The girl, less assiduous now, it's true, would come back without warning when she and Douglas decided to take a break from their manual labours. She labelled jars of ointment, brought new plants to pack into the drying shed with its piles of odours and colours. She helped Mercedes grind seeds and take an inventory. She made her talk about her childhood and the village, and she asked for news about her cousin the bookkeeping nun. But whenever questions full of innuendo started up, Éléna changed the subject.

When Mercedes had trouble walking because of her elderly bones, she took advantage of her problem to leave her house less often, obliging Éléna to come back more frequently to make the deliveries. Thanks to Douglas's canoe, more and more watertight, it now took them twenty minutes or so to get to the village. Light-heartedly, he would take her there and come back for her with no fear of facing the villagers, who in any case greeted him more confidently now.

"Hey, Starling! You're going to take away our little magician?"

"Only if she agrees," was Douglas's invariable answer, making the men laugh who were helping him to berth.

Life was filled then with reassuring habits. But when autumn was already scattering its last colours, the straight road that Douglas and Éléna had been taking changed direction.

They were going to Rivière-aux-Oies intending to bring back some hens that they'd bought or bartered, depending on the mood of the farmer's wife on Back Road. There was barely enough time to attach the canoe to the teetering dock that bordered the river at the level of the village. Dark faces greeted them. Éléna knew that it was about Mercedes.

"She's expecting you," said a neighbour.

Wanting to make her way quickly to Mercedes' house, at the summit of one of the village's rounded hills, Éléna was overcome by violent nausea.

Death gives no quarter. Éléna found her old guardian in bed, her face grey, nearly translucent, turned towards the window.

Dr. Patenaude was waiting in the room. He whispered a few unencouraging words into the ear of Éléna, who pressed him to leave them alone. When he finally left the room to wait in the kitchen with Douglas, Éléna approached on tiptoe. The usual light in Mercedes' tired eyes was already snuffed out. The pharmacist smiled at her anyway, and Éléna forgot the dying woman's authoritarian nature, her firm-handedness, and her sometimes snappish tone of voice. She lay down on the mattress and delicately took Mercedes' round and shrunken body in her arms.

They exchanged neither confidences nor words of affection. No effusiveness. Mercedes had closed her eyes. Éléna tried to find a way to talk to her about the pharmacy, to allow her to leave in peace without lying, because she had no intention of taking over as Mercedes had hoped she would. But the dying woman stopped her with a weak movement and offered her the gift of her last words:

"Love your Douglas."

As she was falling asleep, Mercedes placed her hand on the belly of Éléna, who left it there until the end. Éléna understood that, in her own way, Mercedes was telling her that she must dare to live.

After Mercedes died, Douglas and Éléna lived in a whirlwind that lasted for three weeks and kept them clinging together. The letter to the Little Sisters of Mount Carmel. The people come from afar to salute their pharmacist one last time. The interment. The reception after the ceremony. The murmured memories.

There were decisions to be made. A great many papers to sign in the office of Notary Gingras. They put the house up for sale. Cleaned out the dispensary and took most of the contents to Dr. Patenaude. Furniture and clothes they gave away. Éléna kept the big book of wild plants. Then, over protests by some of the villagers, they left Rivière-aux-Oies without saying where they were going.

It was not to cast aspersions on Mercedes' memory that they felt joy again. Éléna's belly was imperceptibly growing round and that was enough to make them dream. They could not suppress the wonder that the minute shadow around the navel evoked and which Douglas realized at once was that of a girl.

One December night, he surprised her with a cradle. He was standing with his big lumberjack's body and in his hands was a little bed with perfect arches and with the tree of life carved at the head. Solemnly, he offered it to her with the usual careful words of a man who never talks to say nothing. So that from the very first hours of their lives, their children would know they were loved. So that when Douglas and Éléna rocked them, they would picture the world as beautiful as the oak on the path that Douglas had chosen for them, thinking...

She put down her work and was about to move towards him when she saw the tears in his eyes.

"Thinking of what, Douglas?"

Douglas talked about the happiness kept hidden for so long that in the end you don't know it exists. Then arrives with its dark, curly hair.

"I didn't need anything. Look at me now."

That night, Éléna promised Douglas that she would always be at his side, come what may. They stayed entwined, eating hazelnuts and reading the poems of Emily Dickinson. *When winds take Forests in their Paws the Universe is still.* Around them, all was peaceful.

Apparently the winter was dreadful. Snug in their cramped little house, cloistered around the fire, they were hardly aware of it. The snow came early. They watched it fall through the narrow windows while they talked to the little girl who would be enchanted by the sight of the falling flakes. They imagined her excitement when she discovered the taste of strawberries, the smell of the earth, the texture of the sky in January. They thought about the first sounds she would babble to name the fabulous universe all around them: red cardinal and blue jay, fireweed and silver linden... They put on clarinet recitals for her that imitated the muted sound of the water under ice and the lament of the gusts of wind that made branches creak. Douglas made ariettas that Éléna came to like even more than Mozart's.

They no longer left the woods. The bare deciduous trees let in more light than any summer could ever create. A few well-tamped paths and warm boots were all that was needed for trapping. Overnight, a cloak of silence had fallen over the forest. You'd have said that all nature was withdrawing to leave room for their pregnancy.

The baby would be called Rose. She began as a wriggling fish whose first signs excited them more than a sky filled with shooting stars. When the little fish began to drum, at first softly, then pounding, soon day and night, against the walls of Éléna's belly, they could literally see the hands, the feet, and the body all curled up that was only awaiting their arms to become calm.

Lying down, Éléna resembled a dune. Then a hill. Then a mountain. Standing, she had become a strange blend of curves that Douglas found magnificent but that she couldn't get used to. Captive of one body inside another, she was sometimes nearly distraught.

It was neither the isolation nor the fact that there was no electric switch, no hot water tap. If she tried to talk about it, words could not convey what she was feeling. Éléna recalled confusedly the death of her mother and that of old Mercedes, she was already worried about the suffering that Rose would experience, she didn't know if she would be able to protect her against violence and wickedness. Douglas did his best to stay calm. He became even more thoughtful towards her, and he showered her with admiration and affection. While his thoughtfulness touched Éléna, it never allowed her totally to shed the darkness and pigheadedness from her nature.

Starting in June, Rose could arrive at any moment. While there had never been any talk about going back to Rivière-aux-Oies for the delivery, they did bring up the possibility of seeing Dr. Patenaude when the river was open again. Éléna didn't know yet if it would be useful. They would see.

The days passed, they were longing to see, and that was presumptuous. The fine weather was just beginning to fulfill its promises and the month of May turned what was left of the snow around the cabin into a stream. Éléna woke with a start early in the night, not knowing what was happening to her. It wasn't a kick by Rose. On the contrary, the child seemed surprisingly calm. It was infinitely more painful, as if a dull knife were chopping her into tiny pieces.

Éléna was shivering. She lifted the covers and tried to get up. A dark sea was spreading over the sheet. She cried out like a warrior for Douglas to save her and Rose from this shipwreck.

He lit a fire that danced weirdly over the walls of the room. She got used to the pain. Douglas moved away, she made out sounds and, at intervals, realized he was at her side again. Her belly had become a volcano. With all her strength, she followed the shocks that projected Rose out of her body.

It was fast. Like a tropical storm, the gale ended as abruptly as it had come. Éléna heard Rose cry out that she had come into the world, she had time to see Douglas's triumphant smile and the tiny little red-faced girl squirming in his big hands. But when he looked up, Douglas knew at once that something was wrong.

Wide Shot

With its undulating landscape, its old houses scattered as if by the wind, and the shifting mood of its waterway, Rivière-aux-Oies was like a secret divulged by no one lest it round up wolves that would crush it without even noticing. Living there was related to an odd coincidence that no history book would bother to explain. Several generations had followed one another, brought there by an appetite for liberty, and had taken root because of one love story or another. The men's resourcefulness and the women's courage had taken them through a century with no disagreements. The fact that electricity and the telephone had taken so long to find them, and that the road had never taken the trouble to connect them with the rest of the country...no one minded. Protected by its forest, nourished by the river, the village let itself be lulled by seasons at least as moody as its inhabitants.

The decision to settle in Rivière-aux-Oies after medical school may not have fulfilled the expectations for the promising student Léandre Patenaude had been, but it was salutary. He felt more useful there than in a research laboratory, to which his university career would ordinarily have led him. As well, his deliberately chosen exile, though it was a sudden whim, let him escape with elegance the howling of the world.

Eight hundred and twenty-three inhabitants, roughly the same number scattered over a radius of a few kilometres, as well as a vacation clientele in the summer. All swore undying loyalty to Dr. Patenaude, generously fulfilling his professional ambitions. Of course, a quiet life in an out-of-the-way countryside held few tremendous medical challenges and his practice consisted mainly of reassuring pregnant women, being at the bedside of the dying, vaccinating children, or treating their measles and colds. The great epidemics didn't travel to Rivière-aux-Oies, and in any case people no longer died of tuberculosis. Still, a serious fracture, a case of appendicitis, or some accidental tragedy allowed Léandre to bone up enthusiastically on his medical textbooks.

The doctor's house, as the inhabitants of Rivière-aux-Oies called it with a hint of pride, was not particularly charming, but it had the advantage of being central and very big. Léandre Patenaude had set up a dispensary on the ground floor and, lacking imagination, was content to occupy two of the upstairs rooms.

As he was a bachelor, all the young girls in the village had rushed to his place during his first week there. Their pretext was a vague ache or some malaise that might have suggested to him a mysterious infection (and led him to believe that, on his own, he would never be up to the task), but they turned out to have no cause but curiosity. The girls' charm meant nothing: Léandre Patenaude, though always courteous, remained stony-faced. At age twenty-nine, he had not yet found a four-leaf clover and he had no illusions about life's generosity or the surprises it was supposed to have in store. Life, he said, had planned nothing special for him.

The doctor had been living in Rivière-aux-Oies for some years when he noticed Éléna Tavernier's thick, curly hair for the first time. He had been measuring Monsieur Blain the shoemaker's eyeballs, whose goitre seemed finally to have stabilized, when Léandre heard a cheerful voice behind him asking where to put the box of ointments Mercedes had prepared. He hadn't heard her come in and her sudden appearance in his office when he was with a patient annoyed him intensely. About to inform this insolent person, he turned abruptly. At the sight of her, he couldn't say a word.

With a mocking expression, Éléna looked at the hand that was holding a tongue depressor in mid-air above Monsieur Blain's open mouth.

"Shall I put them in the closet?"

The doctor's silence was becoming uncomfortable.

"Umm, no. Please wait outside, Mademoiselle...?"

She left without replying. The shoemaker hastened to inform Léandre that the girl was living at the apothecary's. She was called the Magician, she came from the south, not much was known about her. But at least she wasn't a show-off like the schoolmistress (that Gabrielle Shmoo, who came from the old countries), who he assumed would leave Rivière-aux-Oies before long. When the doctor realized that he wouldn't learn much else about the newcomer, he finished up with his patient and followed him, fearing that Éléna had already left. A few curious faces were watching from the waiting room.

She was sitting quietly on the gallery. They introduced themselves and exchanged small talk. The ointments were made of chickweed and camomile, and there was another with a base of plantain. Yes, she liked the place. No, she hadn't visited the region yet. Well, she had to leave now. Goodbye. The conversation hadn't lasted five minutes. Éléna was practically still a child. Léandre Patenaude was twice her age. Nevertheless, he had fallen in love.

If there had been even a hint of intimacy between Léandre Patenaude and Éléna Tavernier, it was only in the unhappy doctor's dreams. Seeing Éléna had become an obsession.

He began to prepare for her visits by rehearsing what he would say and imagining a scenario with an unlikely dénouement. Alas, whenever she delivered medicine, he found the parcel by the door with a note scrawled on a bit of paper that he reread several times, seeking unsuccessfully some encouraging sign. He changed his habits, tried to match his schedule to hers, to be in the store or at the post office at the right moment, but Éléna was unpredictable, and while they passed each other now and then, they never met. He invited Mercedes for supper at his place, insisting that she bring her protégée; the pharmacist turned up on her own, and he was so disappointed that he let the ham stick to the vegetables in the bottom of the casserole and drank most of the bottle of wine by himself. He also bought a bicycle in the hope of running into Éléna on the road where he'd heard that she went for a ride every day; chance did not play in his favour.

Then, one violently stormy night, Mercedes summoned him to the young girl's bedside. He rushed there, arrived soaking wet, stumbled on the stairs, bruised his forehead, and was so perturbed to see Éléna lying in a bed too big for her that he dared not even touch her. He phoned every day to ask about her. After that, Éléna

Tavernier was not so present in Rivière-aux-Oies, and if by a stroke of luck he finally saw her, he had to admit that she showed no interest in him. When she disappeared almost completely from the village, he dared not ask what had happened.

Mercedes died a year and a half later, and Léandre Patenaude felt his heart crumble when he spotted Éléna with the bearded biologist. Though she was in mourning, the magician was transformed: more mature, calm, and without a doubt loved. The doctor wept so much during the burial that everyone was astonished to discover only now how attached he was to the deceased.

In the village, where nothing escaped the greed for gossip, people noticed that the doctor had become moody. There would be a slight delay in reacting to greetings, a distant gaze during conversations, unusual refusals of invitations to have a beer with the men, to play softball, or to go for a Sunday drive.

In his office, he showed signs of jumpiness and impatience. One woman was rebuffed for forgetting to take her pills. Another suffered Léandre's anger over a badly applied dressing. It was even said that it had taken him three tries to get a simple blood sample (but, strangely, no one remembered the name of the patient to whom it was supposed to have happened). In a few weeks, Léandre Patenaude, already the object of a huge appetite for curiosity, became the main topic of conversation.

The conclusion was that he was considering leaving Rivière-aux-Oies, and without having to discuss at length what their attitude should be, each of them doubled his or her kindness towards the doctor. He seemed not to notice.

Two or three times a year, Léandre Patenaude would be roused from sleep by a knock on his door. But he will say (much) later that, before that night, he'd never heard pounding so fierce. Obviously, he raced to open it, in crumpled pyjamas and bare feet, and he was staggered by what he saw. Douglas Starling was standing on the doorstep, huge, his clothes all bloody, face sweating, eyes bulging. So much so that at first the doctor thought the big man wanted help for himself. Until he noticed the inert body in the giant's arms.

"Do something, Doctor, you have to do something!"

They laid Éléna's body, wrapped in a stained sheet, on one of the two makeshift cots in the doctor's office. Douglas, very agitated, was sobbing. Léandre searched in his black bag, wiped his forehead, hunted for his stethoscope, and tried to stop the trembling in his hands. Part of this was for show, because a trained eye such as his was able to recognize that the young woman was dead. But he went on, discreetly lifted the blood-soaked sheet and slowly listened to her unmoving chest, at the same time asking questions that Douglas answered by fits and starts.

The bleeding must have started during the birth. The heart was not beating. The doctor, whose tears kept him from seeing properly, took the stethoscope tubes from his ears and turned towards Douglas.

"Where is the child?"

Despite the darkness, the sky was clear. Guided by the nearly full moon, the distraught doctor ran across the sleeping village, his dressing gown open. Éléna was only twenty years old. If he had been able to hold on to her, if he'd been more enterprising, if he hadn't let her leave with this...this...Léandre Patenaude's mind was stuck in a nauseating blend of emotions dominated by despair. He ran faster.

At the edge of the water, he found the canoe, its hull wedged between the posts of the dock and the rocks on shore while the stern was swaying in the backwash. Léandre, bent double, hands on his knees, was getting his breath back while his eyes searched the inside of the craft. In the very bottom, wrapped up in her little oak bed, Rose was waiting for him in silence.

At the doctor's house, there was a light on all night. The two men weren't talking. Now and then you could hear Douglas's sobbing, barely audible, and the baby's, which sounded like the squeaking of a young hare. The infant, though puny, grew animated and even seemed to be hanging on. Douglas, though, afraid to see her die in turn, hardly looked at his daughter. With meticulous care, he brushed Éléna's hair, slowly washed her body, and wrapped her in a clean sheet.

Meanwhile, Léandre, with the same maniacal care, was tending the baby. He cleaned her eyes carefully, inserted drops, wiped off the tiny body, powdered it, dressed the umbilical cord, regularly noted pulse and temperature, and examined thoroughly the skin, the limbs, the reflexes, noting everything. Then he diapered her in a cotton tablecloth he'd found in the kitchen and warmed in the oven. He rocked her for a moment before handing her to Douglas, who was still standing beside Éléna, holding her lifeless hand.

"Keep her."

Because he wasn't sure that he'd understood, Léandre did not move, still holding out the sleeping baby to her father. Seeing the doctor's hesitation, Douglas, his beard drenched in tears, turned to him and said in a near whisper:

"Please."

After laying the baby in her cradle, Léandre turned towards Douglas, in whose shadow he could see the pale and quiet face of Éléna. To avoid being carried away in turn by emotion, he cleared his throat and made an effort to go back to the father. Douglas wiped his eyes on his shirt sleeve. Then Léandre saw him lift Éléna, make his way to the door, and open it.

"What are you doing?"

Douglas did not reply, but before disappearing, he turned around one last time.

"Her name is Rose."

The day was spent digging. Douglas chose the middle of the clearing to bury Éléna, across from the house, very close to where the vegetable garden usually was. Fastened to his shovel like a castaway to the only reef in the ocean, he extracted from deep down in the ground, where it was still frozen in places, heaps of earth and pebbles that he arranged around the grave.

When the walls seemed perfectly squared, he lined them with fir boughs. Then he took Éléna from the log cabin and laid her in the grave, her face turned towards the tamaracks at the end of the clearing. He lay down beside her for a moment, and if there had been witnesses, they'd have thought that the lovers had simply dozed off. When Douglas was too numb to lie there any longer, he uprooted himself and wandered around the grave, then sat beside it. He played the clarinet until evening, only breaking off to moan. It was well into the night before he resolved to bury Éléna's body. First, he unscrewed his instrument, placed it in the leather case, and rested it gently in the arms of his love.

In the house, he worked hard to wash away the last traces of blood. When he had finished, the sun was rising. He went back outside and lay down on the cold earth that covered Éléna. Overwhelmed, he sank into a heavy sleep.

The commotion that was livening up the doctor's house was far from going unnoticed. Léandre had cancelled his appointments and now only opened his office for cases of extreme urgency. The sick would have to be patient.

The most preposterous rumours spread faster than the flu in winter. One, about the permanent closing of the clinic — something dreaded by the population of Rivière-aux-Oies — created a new agitation. It was assumed that an epidemic, undoubtedly a serious one, had struck the village and that the doctor himself was incurably ill and had to restrict his activities and impose a quarantine. Or the house was infested by a rare breed of cockroach, something that had happened before, but how then to explain why he'd bought such huge amounts of talcum powder? Could an insect invasion be treated with baby powder?

"His lights are on practically all night."

"If you ask me, he entertains young ladies and you'd be well advised to keep a close eye on your daughters."

"He does it in hiding, he's certainly not offering them a wedding in white!"

(And so on and so forth.)

When Rose's lungs had expanded and one neighbour thought he'd heard a baby cry, the whole village, for once, was flabbergasted.

Léandre's internship in pediatrics was only a vague memory, and the doctor felt that he was not at all prepared to take in a newborn, even if she showed none of the most worrisome signs of prematurity and even if this unexpected custody would be temporary. Distraught, he got organized as best he could.

At birth, Rose weighed a bit over two kilos and slept, at most, for a few hours at a time. During those brief moments of respite, Léandre was busier than he'd have been in the ER of a Chicago hospital. He emptied of its sundry contents one of the unused locked rooms upstairs, adjacent to his own bedroom, and put in what he thought was needed for the well-being of a babe in arms. From the closet in his office where he kept emergency supplies, he took out all the baby's bottles and formula and ordered more in huge quantities. Through the presbytery, he got diapers, a layette, and clothes too big now but that he didn't exchange, thinking that Douglas would be happy to see them last for several months.

Rose was tiny but tough, and demanding. Léandre anxiously counted the hours before Douglas would come back. He opened the door without a word to those who knocked. Disappointment was inscribed in each of the wrinkles that creased his tired eyes. He kept up that rhythm for two weeks.

There were never many pupils at the only school in Rivière-aux-Oies, whose often illiterate parents saw no need to send them for very long. Or teachers, who stopped work to get married, one after another. The arrival of Gabrielle Schmulewitz, whose unpronounceable family name and peculiar accent did nothing to make life easier for her in Rivière-aux-Oies, didn't attract crowds. With as many diplomas as a university professor (but who cared), the teacher persevered nonetheless in getting the most gifted children in the village through their primary and secondary classes.

Numerous parents, even those most inclined to want to hang the diploma of an offspring on the living room wall, were reluctant to entrust their children to a woman whose speech was unfamiliar and background obscure. Especially because she wasn't seen at church. Father Simon had had to intervene from the pulpit to explain, when the teacher was appointed, that Gabrielle was not Christian, so they couldn't force her to sing the glory of the *Patrem omnipotentem* every Sunday. He would teach catechism himself. For the rest, it was Gabrielle or close the school. "In the absence of wheat, we'll eat oats," the *curé* had concluded at the end of his homily, and the parishioners, perplexed, had nonetheless understood that the Church was giving its blessing to the stranger's presence in the village school. The shoemaker, Georges Blain, had been wrong, then. Gabrielle Schmulewitz — Mademoiselle

Shmoo for most people — had no intention of leaving. Between her rented room at Madame Normand's and the school, she went on living a discreet life but would be well advised not to make a hint of a ripple.

Léandre was probably one of the rare individuals to have solved the mystery of the teacher's past. The first time she had consulted him, about a dislocated wrist, she hadn't wanted him to turn the sleeves of her grey sweater up too high and he'd had to persevere until she finally let him. Six numbers were tattooed in blue on her left forearm, which she nervously covered with her hand. 159672.

"What's that?" was the candid question from Léandre, who still knew little about the death camps.

Without replying, she quickly covered her arm before he asked any more questions. Léandre hadn't insisted, but he knew how to read between the lines. This woman, marked like cattle, provoked respect. She was the one whom he asked for help when fate entrusted him with the care of a newborn.

Gabrielle saved Léandre's life, and possibly Rose's as well. She knew how to put the baby to sleep, change her, give her the bottle, burp her, and sing her Jewish lullabies. Léandre didn't hesitate: he suggested that she leave the tiny, unheated room that Madame Normand rented much too expensively and move to his house.

"Free. With no ulterior motive. We're too old anyway. That is, I am. I mean, I'm too old."

She was ten years older. He began to splutter.

"You understand what I'm trying to say, don't you? Take some time to think it over before you say no, Gabrielle. I guarantee that two adults will be none too many to pacify that little fury."

Gabrielle agreed that it would be more practical, and in spite of the terrible fuss that rang out in the village, the very next day she brought over her old suitcase and her five cartons of books. They didn't have time to analyze the rough patches involved in living under the same roof. Until classes were over, Léandre took care of weeknights and Gabrielle, Friday and Saturday. They shared the kitchen, the living room, and the infant's room, sometimes treating themselves (especially Léandre, truth be told) to a glass of Scotch and, when they weren't too exhausted, to conversations that adroitly sealed their friendship. As for the rest, each one adapted to the other's independence and they appreciated the fact that the house was spacious enough to allow it.

Léandre made fewer house calls, but eventually he reopened his office. There, patients got used to the presence of the baby who slept in the cradle with its perfect arches and, at its head, a carving of the tree of life. Rose interrupted the doctor in his work for the smallest thing. It must be said that Léandre came running at the slightest squeak.

When the child was three months old, the doctor and the teacher called Father Simon to have her baptized. On the dotted line of the form, they wrote "father and mother unknown," and in the space for the baby's name, they wrote: Rose Gabrielle Patenaude.

High-Angle Shot

Douglas slept outside with no regard for the weather, moaning in his sleep, swallowed up by endless nightmares of which he remembered only a feeling of suffocation. Night dissolved over him, even at the brightest part of the day. When he woke up, he wept again, went to Éléna's grave, his face buried in the ground, the dry taste of earth in his mouth, and with a steady urge to vomit his empty stomach. Douglas let himself be numbed by pain.

With burning eyes, he was constantly looking for something but didn't know what it was. Otherwise he did not move, did not jump at the slightest sound, did not nod his head, did not throw his arms up, did not protect himself from rain or from the animals that approached to sniff at him; he didn't even chase away blackflies. He hardly breathed. Entire days went by when he was totally indifferent to everything that was alive. Days of fever of which he would have absolutely no recollection.

It was hunger and thirst that drew Douglas out of his stupor. Without realizing it, he began to crawl to the nearest plants, tearing young leaves off small shrubs, taking mushrooms and moss from the ground, arbitrarily ripping up ferns, rhizomes, trilliums. He would chew furiously until his empty stomach subsided a little. He quenched his thirst in the rivulets that cut across the surroundings, and when he got his strength back, he dragged himself all the way to the river.

When his energy was first renewed, he tried to find a guilty party. He chose his father, his mother, his sister, God, winter, and the forest. Then he was stabbed by the truth: it was he himself. Of course it was because of him that Éléna had flown away, that the hope of the three of them reinventing the world disappeared, that the mysterious beauty of love collapsed. He who didn't know how to do anything properly, who could make harvests rot, who ignited calamity, now howled like a wounded animal, cursing himself.

One day, he finally stopped crying. But he went on tormenting himself with unanswerable questions. No sorrow would be heavier to bear, and though he was very young and should live for a long time yet, all his life he would drag around that weighty shadow.

From invoking her so often, Douglas saw Éléna appear now and then, mostly at dusk. He would be calm as soon as he spied her graceful silhouette. She would hail him from between the branches. She would be coming back from the river in which she had bathed, wringing out her hair, head tilted onto her bare shoulder. She would emerge from the cabin smiling, ready to go berry picking, her basket under her arm. She would water the window boxes, joking because water was spurting all over. She would dance beneath the tamaracks, swirling her skirt. She never talked to him, and she disappeared as soon as he tried to approach her.

Once, she came towards him holding a baby.

The summer dragged on. Douglas ate poorly, slept little, and didn't think very much either. Very emaciated, he had metamorphosed. His scruffy beard and greasy hair would have scared the most reckless passersby. But there were no passersby. The vegetable garden was neglected, as were the house, the flower box, the lean-to, the canoe, the path to the river, and the one that led out of the clearing. The animals tried to take advantage of this disorder to make themselves at home. Douglas chased them away with guttural cries.

Éléna's grave dominated all this disorder. The earth there was level, neat, and combed like a miniature arena. Nothing grew there. Not one leaf, not a scrap of wood, a needle of pine or fir, had time to settle there. No wildflower imparted a scrap of life to this desert. Douglas was the mad guard of an austere graveyard.

After another sleepless night spent outside, lying at the edge of the rectangle of virgin territory, he woke with a start. The first glimmers of daylight illuminated feebly something in the very middle of the sacred ground. Like the lunatic he'd become, Douglas wanted to hurl himself at it, exterminate it on the spot. A flock of blue jays began to make a fuss at the same moment and the angry man turned towards them first, roaring. With silence restored, he stared at the soil of the burial place.

A microscopic bud, not yet a twig, rose shyly before him. Douglas recognized it. It was a shoot of tamarack.

Dissolves

The education and health of the village now depended on how well the teacher and the doctor had slept. After a few disconcerting experiences, word had gone out to all the houses in Rivière-aux-Oies: you were no longer supposed to phone the doctor's house, even in daylight, and in case of emergency you came there and tried to knock on his door very softly.

When he heard a gentle hissing at his door, Léandre went to it, thinking that someone had come to fetch him for a delivery (the Giroux family maybe? or Madame Lépine, though that would be early...) or for a hunting accident, as the season had just opened. It was nearly midnight. He opened the door and was shocked to see Douglas on the gallery. Actually, he guessed rather than recognized who it was. He restrained himself from making any rude remark. The man looked more like an animal than a human being. It seemed like the wrong time to criticize him.

"So, Starling, what brings you here?" he asked more coldly than he would have liked, showing him in. "Have you come for a chat, or do you need a treatment of some kind?"

But Douglas stayed planted in the doorway, unmoving. Léandre had to insist that he take a seat inside. A strong animal smell filled the room when they sat, face to face, in the doctor's big wine-coloured armchairs. Léandre decided that a shower and something to eat were undoubtedly more urgent than explanations, which would come in good time. He took Rose's father upstairs, noting how thin he'd become. He offered him clean towels, shampoo, and a razor. He pushed him into the bathroom and gestured reassuringly to Gabrielle when she stuck her head out her own open doorway.

Taken aback by this surprise visit, Léandre quickly fixed a sandwich and a beer, set them on a tray that he placed on the low table in the living room, and poured himself a Scotch, neat. Then it crossed his mind that Douglas had come for Rose and suddenly he had a stomach ache.

Bending over Rose's cradle, Douglas stroked the sleeping child's curly hair.

"She looks like her, doesn't she?"

Léandre nodded, hesitant.

Going downstairs a few minutes later, Douglas merely thanked the doctor for taking care of his daughter. He had walked so he wouldn't be seen and he still had a long way to go. Léandre offered his rarely used bike, which was gathering dust in the shed. Yes, yes, of course Douglas could come back to see the baby now and then. Which night was best for him? Very well, let's say Monday, the people in Rivière-aux-Oies go to bed early on Monday. The last Monday in the month, yes, fine, perfect.

Douglas left just before one a.m. As he closed the door, Léandre felt nearly happy. With nothing to support it, his usual pessimism was failing. He ran to announce the good news to Gabrielle.

Douglas got into the habit of going to the Schmulewitz-Patenaude home around once a month. In December, a snowstorm kept him from travelling the ten kilometres or so to the doctor's house, but he resumed the following week, arriving unexpectedly with a Christmas present for Rose in his bag: a mobile of which the tiny elements were scale models of six different trees, carved in wood. Tamarack, which he'd dried for two years, he told them. A hard, resilient wood, imputrescible, perhaps the most resistant and heaviest of all. Used in the past for building bridges over streams. Docks, too. With the roots, the Natives used to sew their canoes. And Léandre must know that tamarack bark fought all kinds of infections. Isn't that so, Doctor?

Douglas's hosts couldn't get over it. The silent man who'd had trouble forming a complete sentence during each of his visits was now lively and animated. And he knew the word *imputrescible*.

"I . . . I see that you're feeling better, Douglas," Léandre stammered.

"I don't know. Probably, yes. You see, there's someone giving me a lot of help."

No, the doctor didn't see exactly what Douglas was alluding to, unless it was that his grief had begun to heal. At the time, it was of no consequence.

"That person who's helping me . . . made a suggestion. What if I were to become a forest ranger?"

At first, Léandre disapproved. He was living on land that did not belong to him....

Douglas flared up. "Exactly. My presence in the woods would be legitimate. I wouldn't have to hide. I know that forest better than anyone. I can guarantee to protect it against poaching, fires. Insects too, ones that attack trees—gypsy moths, the pine sawfly, the satin butterfly..."

Léandre coughed. "It's true, you're a biologist."

Douglas didn't blink. "And I could see more of Rose. I'll make a little money, so I'll be able to contribute to the expenses. I'll even be able to rent a room from you. That way I'll be a lot more comfortable showing up without warning. What do you think?"

If enthusiasm hadn't blinded Douglas, he might have noticed the perfectly attuned frowns of Léandre and Gabrielle. Of course, *he could see more of Rose.*

"Look, Douglas, this isn't about money."

"Léandre, Gabrielle! Can't you see that it's a fabulous idea?"

Rose had finished her bottle. Snuggled for the first time in Douglas's arms, where she seemed even smaller than usual, she fell asleep confidently, head against her father's heart, mouth open. Her fists were clutching Douglas's frayed sweater.

Gabrielle insisted. The next day, Dr. Patenaude requested an official meeting with the mayor of

Rivière-aux-Oies to suggest to him Douglas's fabulous idea. He would serve as guarantor for the new forest ranger. And he was so persuasive that, a month later, it was settled. Douglas, though, refused to wear a uniform.

The strange family went outrageously against propriety, and the gossips had an inexhaustible supply of raw material. While some were content to think there was a little too much visiting in the doctor's house, most were still pernickety about the morality of the ties between Léandre, Gabrielle, and Douglas. The village was unanimous, however, on at least one point: it hardly mattered where Rose had come from; if *joie de vivre* had a face, it would be hers.

Of the three adults who bent over Rose's cradle, it was Gabrielle who was transformed most radically by the baby's unexpected arrival. She now allowed a few wisps of hair to escape from her perpetual chignon — including when she appeared in class. Her stiff body had loosened a little, and her pupils had stopped calling her behind her back "Colonel Shovelhead" and "fancy foreigner," a term taken from the adults. Her clothes, until then spotless, were looser now, always crumpled in the same places, and stained with regurgitated milk and sweet almond oil.

Ever since Léandre had asked her to watch over Rose with him, the child had only to gurgle at her in an expression of childish trust and the teacher would smile. People would see her taking the infant for a walk as if she were her own, running along with the stroller while she sang and making faces when the little one opened wide her amused eyes.

"Are you sure you aren't overdoing it, Gabrielle?"

"Are you sure you aren't jealous, Léandre? Here, take her, she's asleep. But be careful with her head."

"I know how to hold a baby."

"So do I. I had a niece, you know. No bigger than Rose..."

Gabrielle opened up in dribs and drabs, and Léandre collected her confidences with ambassadorial tact. He didn't rush her. He tried to piece her story together backwards, from Rivière-aux-Oies, which she no longer thought of leaving, and a sanatorium that she could no longer situate; he informed himself about Birkenau, looked up Drancy in an atlas... He put away that confession, which had come out by chance like the others, in the brand new Schmulewitz-Patenaude family album and merely held Rose a little more tightly.

When Gabrielle offered to stop teaching and devote herself entirely to the unexpected baby, Léandre pointed out that if she could wait a few years, she would be the one who would take charge of Rose's education, all day, all year. Nothing seemed more wonderful to Gabrielle than the prospect of spending the whole day, twelve months of the year, with Rose. So she waited, and Léandre was able to keep Rose with him during his office hours.

The child grew up, then, in the midst of syringes and catheters, playing with absorbent cotton and empty pill bottles, and when still in her playpen she would greet patients with a ringing "hurt" filled with compassion that made them laugh.

"My assistant," announced the doctor proudly to anyone who was listening.

It was Rose who called the shots in the big house. It could happen that Léandre's patients found the doctor sweating, going up and down the stairs non-stop with the little girl on his back. Or on hands and knees in the corridor, in the middle of a noisy game of hide-and-seek. Léandre's famous handkerchiefs were used for hardly anything now but wiping off his sweaty neck.

But what made Léandre proudest was that Rose would pretend to read prescriptions long before she took an interest in the picture books that Gabrielle and Douglas were always giving her.

Generally, they talked about Rose — her first words, first tooth, first fever — but inevitably about other things as well. Gabrielle made fritters for them that they dunked in coffee when it was cold or a lemon sherbet they loved during the heat of July. Léandre would bring out his wine and they would drink to their little girl who was growing up normally. Douglas brought maple syrup in the spring, game or fresh fish depending on the season, and, of course, the toys he made for Rose (including a much too pointed spinning top that Gabrielle and Léandre accepted with a smile, not letting their disapproval show).

In spite of his efforts to hide it, Léandre had trouble getting used to Douglas's sporadic presence in the house, and now and then he let his irritation show. Nonetheless, from spending time together, the trio eventually lifted some veils that would suggest they were growing closer.

"My brother was twenty-four when he died, in northern Italy, while I was here looking after men coming home from the front."

"They tore her out of my arms, she started to howl, my sister dropped the suitcases and rushed to take her. I never saw them again."

Douglas did not talk about his family. But occasionally:

"When a pool of sunlight passes through the forest, I sometimes wish that I believed in God."

Not a word about Éléna. Her death was not even evoked on Rose's first birthday. On the other hand, on the child's second birthday, Douglas rushed out of the room when she ran and took refuge in Gabrielle's arms, calling her Maman.

The paths that ran through the forest of Rivière-aux-Oies were packed down. Summer and winter, you now had to want to get lost pretty badly. They were easy to walk on, but everyone who ventured there — hikers, hunters, and berry-pickers — was warned that they mustn't go beyond a certain point and that the forest ranger would be quick to warn them if they didn't respect the notices put up for that purpose. In fact, so far, no one had been able to approach Douglas's sanctuary.

Éléna's grave was surrounded by a low wall made of golden polished wood as soft as silk velvet. In place of a headstone, the tamarack was already no longer a shrub. Its light branches stood well above the enclosure. Lovingly protected by Douglas, who watered it nearly every day during the hot season, loosening the soil and feeding it compost, the tree would live for a thousand years, one day attain a height of sixty metres, and Éléna would soar towards the light and tower over the whole forest.

"You don't seem to understand what I'm saying: she has come back! I talk to her every day."

Léandre couldn't stop himself from rolling his eyes, but the next day he took advantage of the fact that Éléna had slipped into the conversation to satisfy his own curiosity. Gabrielle pricked up her ears. What was most important to her was to ensure that the Tavernier family would not try to snatch Rose away from her one day. The reply to a discreetly sent letter reassured her: the last

Taverniers in Saint-Lupien had been dead for years. Her fears appeased now, on the pretext of some chore or other she left Douglas and Léandre alone more and more often to bring out their memories. Better than anyone, Gabrielle understood the importance of praising the dead.

"She never said anything about me?" Léandre dared to ask one day when they were alone.

"Sure, she and Mercedes had nicknamed you Pressing Cloth," Douglas was about to reply in a jocular tone, and would have added spontaneously that Éléna had said he looked stiff. But he stopped himself in time when he saw the doctor regard him anxiously, instead making up as he was telling it a natural current of friendship between the young dead woman and the doctor. As for Léandre, he steered clear of explaining that monitoring by a doctor would most likely have made possible a quick diagnosis, and he donned several pairs of kid gloves to assure Douglas that Éléna's death —

"But Éléna isn't dead!" Douglas interrupted him, putting his hand on the doctor's arm.

No, of course not, thought Léandre sadly.

While he wasn't interested in the details of the laws and preventive measures he was asked to apply, Douglas was getting along fairly well. He proceeded by hunch and was rarely wrong. Lying in wait for the slightest sign of damage or danger, he terrified potential offenders by threatening them with the harshest kind of cruel treatment. So much so that for the years when he was forest ranger, there were few serious offences to report to the authorities. His work gave him permission to rule supreme over the forest.

In Rivière-aux-Oies, his unorthodox methods initially provoked a light but steady stream of complaints. That stopped, though, when the village saw the arrival in fits and starts of new hordes of vacationers, exhausted urbanites in search of a place with a bit of shade and water where they could spend their savings. An unexpected godsend. A bed-and-breakfast, then an inn or a campsite began to appear unannounced just before summer. Twice, the dock was enlarged. Some villagers suddenly became expert anglers or hunting guides. The general store started selling athletic gear as well as dried branches tied with purple raffia, pebbles glued to little boards, industrial ashtrays, and cups with a photo of the approach to the village imprinted in washed-out colours.

Douglas's work became tedious, particularly from June to October, a period he would have preferred to spend taking an inventory of the trees and marking them instead of flushing out dazed campers and foolhardy boaters. Now Gabrielle and Léandre saw him arrive tired, rushed, and crabby. ("At least it's a change from his gloom," Gabrielle told Léandre, who'd been complaining.) But Léandre could no longer cope with his work on his own either, and had to hire a nurse to help him during the summer rush. The constant traffic in and out of the house during the loveliest time of the year pleased no one, and their evenings now ended in long arguments during which they observed together that the quiet life as they'd known it until then was in the process of abandoning them.

"A shopping centre? What's that?"

Gabrielle had just explained to Douglas why, at the edge of the forest, a rectangle longer than a football field had been surrounded that very day with yellow tape and some huge placards that read No Admittance. A businessman had made a great impression on the mayor, a powerful and determined businessman. Convincing, too, because the mayor was very excited. An enormous grocery store. There was even talk of ten stores, while for the time being Rivière-aux-Oies had only one and a half. And all those construction jobs... An arsenal of cranes and cement mixers was expected in a matter of days.

"And why not a four-lane boulevard, a six-storey hotel, and waterslides?" asked Léandre ironically.

Gabrielle burst out laughing, but Douglas was pensive.

During the three months the shopping centre's construction lasted, Douglas stayed hidden away in the forest. The weather was cool and rainy, gloomier than usual, and walkers were rare. The forest ranger took advantage of it to spend all his time with Éléna. Always close to the tamarack tree, he wrapped himself in the blankets she had sewn and reassured himself, his nose in one of her old sweaters, the letters written on birch bark within reach. He talked to her while waiting for a trout to bite; while weather-stripping the cabin door to make it mouse-proof; and even when he had to shut himself inside the cabin because the nights were too cold to sleep outside. He told her about the progress of Rose, who had just turned five, describing the child's affection for Léandre and Gabrielle. "She marvels at everything you wanted us to show her," he whispered at the foot of the tree. "She loves the taste of strawberries and the smell of the earth."

Douglas was nervous, though. His father's shadow in the neighbourhood and the bad omens that accompanied it terrified him. His imagination went into overdrive, misfortune scoffed at him. That summer, in spite of wind and rain, he never heated the log cabin, fearing that a curl of smoke might guide Antoine Brady to him. He was cold and he ate his fish raw. He kept quiet, content to pace the boundaries of his clearing. He tried not to panic and asked Éléna what he should do. Stroking the needles of the tamarack, he listened to the answer of the wind.

In Douglas's absence, Gabrielle and Rose were faithful visitors to the parish library, where it was hard to find anything but religious texts among the thousand books on the shelves. One day when she was leafing through an essay by Teilhard de Chardin, Gabrielle was accosted by the village veterinarian, father of two of her pupils. He spoke very softly.

"I thought you were Jewish."

She retorted:

"Jews are capable of reading, you know."

"Don't take it wrong. I was wondering what it was about Teilhard de Chardin that interests you."

"I was hesitating between *The Edifying Life of Saint Ribert* and that of Saint Gudula. They made Teilhard seem fascinating."

Jérôme Fortier smiled and whispered in her ear that he had the complete works of Balzac and of Émile Zola and of many other authors on the Index that he would be happy to lend her if she'd have a coffee with him. Looking at the little girl who was clinging to Gabrielle's skirt, he added:

"I also have a very fine illustrated *Alice in Wonderland.*"

Unaccustomed to being courted, Gabrielle quickly tucked away some locks of hair while she improvised on the neutral theme of white rabbits wearing waistcoats and always in a hurry. She had the impression, though, that she would enjoy a coffee.

Gabrielle was often out when the school holidays should have kept her in the kitchen, Léandre thought. When he closed his office, he no longer smelled the aroma of pork chops or braised beef, and now he found a brief note directing him to leftovers in the fridge. The house was empty.

She went out with Rose, who caught a cold and had frequent earaches, and Léandre kept them both inside for a week. Even during that week, though, when things could have come back to normal, the climate in the family was strained.

"Isn't she a little young for *Alice in Wonderland*?"

Gabrielle, smiling more than ever, ignored his remarks. She grew distant and even more secretive. Léandre took it particularly hard because the construction site, with its nearly daily accidents, was unfortunately creating too much work for him and he couldn't find a nurse, or even a nurse's aide, to assist him that summer.

For the second time in his life, Léandre began to look forward impatiently to the return of Douglas. One Sunday, exasperated, he decided to look for him in the forest and bring him back to the house. But the directions were too vague and he came home empty-handed after an hour, grouchier than when he'd set out. The summer was interminable.

When Gabrielle spoke to her pupils about acts of kindness, she knew whereof she spoke. Her life, like Léandre's, had been a winding path that had led her to believe that everything, always, would have the insipid taste of duty. She'd had to take many detours before she came to Rose. But when Jérôme Fortier took her in his arms, Gabrielle was overcome by vertigo, dazzled by the thought that perfection had now chosen to take over her fate. To be loved utterly like that was far more fulfilling than what she believed herself authorized to dream of. She discovered a sudden interest in the vaccination of poultry and equine dermatitis.

Halfway through the race, however, Gabrielle realized that it was unlikely she would be able to have her cake and eat it. It was Jérôme Fortier himself who, in spite of charm and intelligence, in spite of novels wrapped in brown paper and bouquets of flowers delivered to the house, solidly drove in the nail that put an end to the dream.

"Let's get married!"

They had known each other for just a few weeks. That day, she burst out laughing, which he found offensive.

"Move in with me. I can rent you a room too. You'll see, the girls will be thrilled."

She was not at all certain, and on this other day she was content to joke.

"You never spend more than two consecutive hours with me. You go back and forth between his place and mine. People are talking."

That was the least of Gabrielle's concerns. She explained it patiently to him.

"Rose, Rose, Rose! She's not even your daughter!"

That night, Gabrielle grabbed her purse, put on her coat, and left the room, leaving her umbrella behind in the front closet. She never came back for it.

They were at the table, eating dinner in silence.
Construction of the shopping centre had been finished
for a week and Léandre was working less overtime.
The resumption of school forced Gabrielle to spend her
evenings preparing her classes, so she didn't go out. Rose,
now a boisterous five-year-old, was still adorable but
devoured a lot of energy. They were tired.

The little girl raised her curly head towards the adults
and wrinkled her nose over her plate, asking how come
she had zero sisters and Jean-Charles had three? They had
always agreed to tell her the truth, but all at once Léandre
and Gabrielle were talking at the same time and it was
impossible to understand what they were trying to say.
Rose looked at them, skeptical.

"Would you like to have a sister?" Gabrielle asked.

The question was not mischievous, but it chilled
Léandre's blood and his eyes were heavy with innuendo.
Gabrielle blushed, imagining the hyperactive silhouettes
of Jérôme Fortier's daughters. She hadn't seen him since
the night of the umbrella. She didn't have time to get
angry: Rose was looking hard at them with her special
smile, declaring that she'd rather have a talking rabbit.

They laughed awkwardly, ill at ease.

"You and I have to talk about it," Léandre grumbled,
peering at Gabrielle, who hurried to clear the table.

It was at precisely that moment that Douglas chose to
show up, asking happily if there was a five-year-old little

girl in this house and if she missed her papa. Rose got up from the table as quickly as she could, knocking over her chair and shrieking:

"I'm getting a bunny, I'm getting a bunny!"

The hugging and kissing were of short duration because Léandre's anger exploded and headed straight for Douglas.

"So now you're back? You're gone for three months without a word and you think you can just stop by whenever it pleases you?"

Douglas put Rose down and tried to explain, but Léandre went berserk. He did so with unusual virulence, using words that preceded his thoughts by several kilometres. Douglas listened, stunned, to Léandre's rancour, then to Gabrielle's efforts to calm him.

"Leave me alone, Gabrielle. Why don't you go and see your widower who babysits sick cows?"

Gabrielle was able to fan the flames in turn by launching into a tirade of which no one would have thought her capable. She hadn't entered the priesthood, she had the right to a private life, a love life if it appealed to her, the veterinarian was an intelligent man, he had charm, Rose was fond of him—

"What?"

They had roared in unison, but Douglas was quicker and let out the only remark he could make loud enough for everyone to hear.

"Rose already has a father and it's me."

"Let's just talk about what fatherhood means to you."

This time, Léandre turned bad-tempered, confusing everything. His love for Éléna. His love for Rose. And Douglas constantly in his way… The quarrel got out of hand and voices went up a notch. The hostilities were going around in circles, on and on. Then:

"You let your wife die in the middle of the woods and you claim you can look after a little girl?"

There was an awkward pause and they heard Rose sobbing, sitting on a step with both hands clutching the banister. The war ended then and there.

Douglas ran to the kitchen to fix a hot chocolate because he knew it would calm Rose quickly. Meanwhile, Gabrielle rushed to console the little girl and Léandre began to clown around to cheer her up. When Douglas came back a few minutes later, he looked at Léandre and Gabrielle bending over Rose on the stairs. The child was sniffling, but she'd stopped crying, Gabrielle's arm was around her as she told her a story about animals who were trying to see which one cried the loudest, while Léandre was stroking her hair and agreeing with Gabrielle's every word.

Douglas set the cup on the low table in the living room and left discreetly.

Douglas's sorrow galvanized him. He rowed vigorously all the way home. In the cabin, he grabbed his clothes and a few objects and stuffed them into his bag. He gathered up his books, tied them into two large compact parcels, and tucked Éléna's letters into them. He packed some food as well and tossed everything into the canoe.

When he came back to the clearing, he looked around his property one last time. Everything was peaceful. He walked to the tamarack, knelt in front of it, and wrapped the narrow trunk in his arms.

"We're leaving now, Curly Girl."

First, he broke up the low wall. Then he took the shovel from the lean-to and dug around the tree, very careful not to damage the roots. He dug in the earth, following the broad, wrinkled branches that were tangled up over an amazing length for a tree so young. He used his hands so as not to break anything. He put such care into it that the job took several hours.

When Douglas felt that he had cleared the entire underground network of the tamarack, he held on to the trunk and gently turned it. The tree did not resist. It landed softly on its side, letting the thin branches cushion its fall. Douglas pulled it from the ground. In the tangle of its roots, he recognized the black leather handle of the clarinet case.

The night was dark, and at first Gabrielle could make out nothing of the opaque mass in front of her. Even Douglas's voice was unrecognizable.

"I'm so glad it's you. I swear, Léandre didn't mean a word of what he said."

"I'm leaving."

"Don't be ridiculous. Come in. It was just an argument. Léandre is exhausted. If I know him, he'll apologize tomorrow."

Douglas did not go inside. He handed her the books and the clarinet. "These are for Rose," he said with difficulty. Then, while Gabrielle set the packages on the ground without bothering to see what they were, he explained to her in a feeble voice how to transplant the tree. A big trench. A sunny spot. Behind the house, for instance. Gently. Compost and a little lime. A solid stake for the bottom third of the trunk. The neck of the tree has to be above ground. And water, plenty of water.

Gabrielle, stunned, saw the tamarack lying on the gallery, its roots wrapped in large damp cloths.

"You're out of your mind!"

"Promise you'll do it. Tomorrow. Promise on Rose's head."

"All right. I promise."

Douglas said thanks, quickly embraced her, and was already on his way when Gabrielle tried again to keep him there.

"Won't you even take the time to say goodbye to her?"

"I can't. If I did, I'd take her with me."

Anxious to be done with it, he rushed away while Gabrielle stood in the doorway peering into the darkness. She stayed until she thought she saw Douglas's canoe heading for the river and its estuary.

Fast Motion

After the first shovelful of earth was dug for the foundation of the shopping centre, Antoine Brady never again set foot in Rivière-aux-Oies. But that didn't stop the village from being transformed under his authority. An upheaval that no one noticed at first. It happened gradually, hidden in the electrifying vocabulary of progress. The future, then, belonged to swollen cities. It would never be known if it was the unbroken wave of new arrivals that led to the development of a large sawmill with a smoking cone, massive corrugated iron warehouses, and some specialized factories. Or if the sawmill, warehouses, and factories had been created to make possible the construction of roads with their perpendicular lots and sprinkling of cheap houses, all identical. Unless it was the new houses and the promise to build others that, little by little, attracted all these people from elsewhere who'd come to work in the sawmill, warehouses, and factories.

Still, one morning Rose was the first to notice that she could no longer hear the river from her bedroom window. She jumped out of bed and shot downstairs to tell Léandre and Gabrielle, who were having breakfast in the kitchen. They gazed at her for a moment while she fidgeted. Taller than other girls her age. Face hidden by a shock of curly hair. Sometimes sombre, sometimes theatrical. An unpredictable temperament. She didn't resemble anyone. No doubt that was normal. After all, Rose had two fathers, two mothers, and a tree to form her, and not everyone can claim that.

Douglas didn't come back to Rivière-aux-Oies either, and if he phoned, he didn't speak. But he wrote. Brown envelopes with no return address arrived regularly for Rose. Each contained a notebook, thick or thin, in which he talked about Éléna but also about Mozart, Rimbaud, and Whitman. Restrained prose, written in small letters that completely covered the lined pages.

Aside from Éléna and the artists from another age, humans were rarely mentioned in the notebooks. Instead, and primarily, Douglas described the fir trees that bore his name, ninety metres tall, whose cones covered the ground of an entire island, which confirmed to Léandre and Gabrielle that he'd gone west. Then the world's largest ocean, deep, steep-sided valleys, giant sequoias. Green lakes, blue lagoons, pink flamingos. A string of islands. Mangroves with their roots that rose above the soil. A forest of scrawny bamboos with trunks so tightly aligned that it was impossible to inch one's way through them. And then the sacred baobab, looming out of nowhere... Douglas travelled a lot.

Those trails, but even more the postmarks and stamps, kept carefully in order of arrival in a schoolgirl's scribbler, allowed them to follow Douglas's route. Léandre put a huge map of the world, ordered from *Reader's Digest*, on the wall in Rose's room, on which, all through her childhood, she used a red felt pen to mark the places where her father was.

For some years, Rose received the notebooks as a game that she appeared to find incredibly amusing. But as Douglas's route seemed to be taking him away from Rivière-aux-Oies permanently, she began to dream about roads, on sea or land, that would bring her father back to her. Because, since her fifth birthday, Douglas had missed every Christmas and every one of Rose's birthdays. He had not been present at any of the little school plays in which she participated or at the provincial music festival in which she won first prize. He wasn't there when she broke her leg skating and had to use crutches for most of the winter. He didn't see her grow up and recite by heart poems that she chose to please him, or dress up as a weeping willow for Halloween. He didn't teach her the rudiments of the foreign languages he was starting to master and he did not instill in her any notions of philosophy. He did, however, pass on to her his zeal for nature and, by force of circumstance, he taught her geography.

Léandre could never say no to Rose and this had given rise to lively arguments with Gabrielle.

While it was common knowledge that he was absolutely crazy about his daughter's hair, it was he who agreed to go with her to the hairdresser to have it straightened, a procedure that turned into a disaster but to which he had graciously yielded when the teenaged girl begged him, swearing that nothing else could make her happy. As well, he bought her a hideous frilly green dress that she'd seen in a catalogue and on which she had her heart set, but she never wore it. And once again, it was he who, at great expense, brought a veteran from a neighbouring village who, having once been part of a military brass band, proved to be the only one who could teach Rose the rudiments of the clarinet. When the pupil outshone the master, Léandre gave Rose a piano and was always the most attentive follower of her progress.

The building of a hospital in Rivière-aux-Oies caused Léandre much concern, but it allowed him to take vacations. He devoted every moment of them to Rose, and while generally he couldn't take her where she would have liked ("Mahogany gaboons grow in equatorial Africa. Can we go to Gabon?"), he took her as often as he could to the big city, where he spent fortunes on concert tickets.

On his rare solo expeditions outside Rivière-aux-Oies, to accompany a patient to a larger medical centre or to attend a meeting, he brought home suitcases filled with everything he thought might please his daughter: books of poetry (which he himself never read); music scores (about which he knew nothing); abundantly illustrated atlases (he whose greatest fear was to see her go away to join Douglas). Rose, always moved by Léandre's thoughtfulness, never told him that she already had a copy of Anne Hébert's poems or that the arrangement of the Chopin prelude was too simple for one who had recently mastered the original score. Or that atlases made her sad.

No one could pronounce Gabrielle's surname as well
as Rose. When she said "Schmulewitz," rounding her
voluptuous mouth, one got the impression that she was
reciting a prayer. Gabrielle melted every time and forgot
half of the basic precepts on the education of children.

As long as Rose was young, everything happened
exactly as Dr. Spock predicted, and Gabrielle's
temperament seemed to have been made to measure for
motherhood. But once Douglas had gone, the little girl
grew moody and life became a struggle for Gabrielle.
The much-anticipated year when she would be able to
keep her in school all day, though, had arrived.

Listening to advice from the mothers of certain pupils,
themselves absorbed by their offspring, she thought it
wise, to offset Léandre's negligence, to draw up rules that
Rose was quick to infringe, but always at the limit of the
justifiable. Only one girlfriend at a time in her room, and
Rose would invite one, while others just happened to
drop by a few minutes later. Two hours of homework
every evening and half an hour of piano every day:
Rose reversed the time devoted to books and music and
managed to pass all her exams anyway. The bed made
every morning, and every morning the bed was made,
but the duvet or the pillows were tossed any old way
because "who says that a pillow has to wait for us against
the wall?" Léandre thought it was funny.

Gabrielle was often upset, but she always tried for recon-
ciliation. As Rose got older, she would dig in her heels
and avoided being alone with Gabrielle. She chose a desk
at the back of the classroom. She shut herself away in her
room. She spent hours, summer and winter, under the
tamarack in the garden.

Neither Léandre nor Gabrielle had thought it necessary
to explain to Rose right away that the tamarack was
supposed to represent the unlikely resurrection of Éléna.
They merely said that Douglas had left it as a gift before
he went away. They had planted it as he'd requested,
in the centre of the property, behind the house.

The tree was quick to regain its vigour. Mind you,
Rose virtually worshipped it and took care of it more
than other children might a dog or a cat. Her everyday life
was punctuated with bone meal and watering. The girl
plunged into the *Encyclopaedia Britannica* as if it were a
horticultural guide. She kept up an epistolary relationship,
brief but intense, with the Farmwives' Circle in the next
village in order to worm out of them some techniques for
layering. She spent hours wearing out her eyes on pictures
of scales and cones that she wanted to be sure she could
identify.

Although not the slightest encouragement had been
expressed, the tamarack assumed a disproportionate place
in Rose's life as she ran out to greet it before and after
school and spent long afternoons with it during her

holidays. Meanwhile, Gabrielle had to be content with small motherly rituals such as birthday balloons to blow up, Rose's bedroom to tidy, hems to sew, and chocolate icing. What with the new school and the young teachers who were arriving as reinforcements, she was snowed under. The lifting of the ban on certain books and the establishment of a library kept her very busy too. Saturday, though, between her ironing board and her classic cookbook *La cuisine raisonnée*, Gabrielle waited in silence for the moment when she would once again become friends with her daughter.

"Why are you giving me all that stuff? What is it? Birch bark?"

"They're letters your mother wrote to Douglas."

"My real mother?"

Gabrielle felt a pang.

"Yes. Letters from Éléna, your real mother."

Gabrielle wanted to suggest that they read them together, but Rose had already run off with the bundle —behind the house, of course. Gabrielle contented herself with observing her from the kitchen, as was now her habit. The girl had her back against the tamarack. She used both hands to unroll the dry pieces of bark, careful not to break them.

Leaning on the kitchen counter, Gabrielle spied on Rose through the window until she'd read all the letters. Then she joined her.

"Don't be sad," she said, sitting on the ground next to her daughter. "Those we love never leave us."

For twenty-five years, Gabrielle had silenced a good number of her most painful memories and refused to read testimonies or to see films about the Shoah. Television had never interested her. She had always found it hard to look into the eyes of people she didn't know when they were introduced. She still had a phobia about dogs and could not stay calm in the face of shouting, especially if it came from a crowd. The siren of the freight train that henceforth went past twice a day on the other side of the river made her shudder every time, whatever the season. She told Rose all of that.

Then, gently, she explained why, more than anything else in the world, she hated the grey smoke from the sawmill.

"You know, Rose, I loved your mother too," Léandre told her some time afterwards.

It was not that Rose doubted Léandre's sincerity. She looked at him through half-closed eyes, trying to imagine the vigorous young doctor who could have charmed Éléna. It was hard.

"Have you got a photo of her?"

"No."

"Was she pretty?"

"Very pretty. Her hair was like yours, but black. She also had your smile, and she was vivacious and independent. Like you."

"Really? You think I look like her?"

Now there were long conversations during which father and daughter together recalled someone neither of them had really known. Gabrielle was silent and listened closely, accustomed to living next to Éléna. But the day Rose wanted to know where her mother was buried, the explanations of both Léandre and Gabrielle were too evasive for the young girl to be content with.

The more Rivière-aux-Oies expanded, the more its forest receded, eaten up first by the shopping centre and then by other structures, all of which looked like hangars. In contrast, in the area near the road, which still followed the river for dozens of kilometres, nothing seemed to have changed except that the dirt road was now asphalt, wider, and busier.

"It should be right about here," said Léandre as he parked the old Volvo on the shoulder.

They got out of the car, surprised by the biting autumn wind that was making the leaves swirl in a sunless sky. Rose was holding tight to a bouquet of white flowers bought before they left. Her parents put on a bold front by chattering away as if it were an ordinary drive. But an oppressive sadness went with them.

No paths invited them to enter. They had to step across a ditch, push aside the bare branches of the June-berry trees to make their way through the firs. Gabrielle was beginning to regret the expedition, but before she dared show her apprehension, Léandre had already started to plot their way. They rushed into it in single file and didn't have to struggle very long. After just a few metres, Rose and Gabrielle heard Léandre come out with a resounding oath.

They found themselves not in an increasingly dense forest but in an arid steppe where lumps of soil, roots, dry branches, and dead wood were all jumbled together. Here and there, a scrawny trunk was still standing. Between the ruts left by trucks of at least forty tons, judging by the tire tracks, stood hundreds and hundreds of wide stumps. Every one was a scar, a small stool waiting for spectators.

But to look at what? It could have been sterile earth. Pine trees, firs, maples, birch, oak, aspen—all had been razed to the ground and laid down in tall, scattered piles.

Paralyzed, they gazed in silence at the devastation of the landscape that stretched out as far as the eye could see. The wind, more aggressive than on the empty plain, added to the already lugubrious atmosphere. In spite of the cold, they advanced along the sodden soil, walking around the clods of earth and the tree trunks. They went in different directions, eyes glued to the sawdust-covered ground. As if some clue or other were suddenly going to give some meaning to their expedition.

Without knowing it, they might even have been walking on Éléna's remains. Rose had to resign herself to placing her flowers at random, somewhere in the middle of a gigantic graveyard.

Music

Douglas explored the planet. He came up against the violence of lunatics and their wars, whether they lasted six days or six years. He visited countries suffering famine and destitution and others so obese that they slept with their noses in the garbage can. But everywhere, and with the same spirit, he did his utmost to track down perfection and make a gift of it to Rose.

His notebooks, diligently written, gave him the illusion of a never-interrupted relationship with his daughter. There were times, however, when he couldn't resist the urge to at least hear her voice. More than once, when his savings allowed, he would pounce on a phone booth and dial the number of the house in Rivière-aux-Oies, but Rose never answered. Léandre would pick up. Douglas disconnected.

The entire world offered Douglas Starling a multitude of skinny young women with curly black hair under whose skirts he could pretend now and then. Nights in cheap hotels could only disperse the mirage. With his burden of grief, he didn't learn how to recover memories.

One night, lying in the dormitory in the hold where he rarely fell asleep, he listened to his shipmates snoring. That was when he made up his mind. The freighter was en route to Melbourne, where he hoped to have time to see the giant eucalyptus trees in Ferntree Gully so he could describe them to Rose. That would be the last travel souvenir he would send her. Right afterwards, he would find a way to go home.

Unlike her parents and the eight hundred and twenty-three persons who were living in Rivière-aux-Oies when Dr. Patenaude had settled there, Rose knew nothing but the frenzied and rapid development of her village. Though she'd taken her first steps in a tiny place in the countryside where the unpredictable climate produced an extraordinary flora, she finished high school in a small industrial town that smelled of sulphur as soon as the wind blew from the east.

One could, at best, get used to the way Rivière-aux-Oies was being defaced, or no longer remember a crossroads or an elm tree that had mattered once. It was another story for the attitudes that went along with the overall mess. Blind greed dragged in its wake upsets to which neither Gabrielle nor Léandre could resign themselves. Without even being aware of it, their affection for Rivière-aux-Oies was now attached only to a very uncertain thread of nostalgia.

The thread broke on the morning when Léandre, just leaving for the hospital, discovered on the front of his gallery hate-filled graffiti directed at Gabrielle. That day, he flew into his most famous explosion of rage and suggested, without thinking it over, that it might be time to sell the house and start over again somewhere else. Gabrielle agreed immediately. As for Rose, she said she would go with them, but "on the condition that you

promise and swear that the tamarack will come too."
Léandre and Gabrielle promised and swore.

Their plan to leave sped up when Rose was invited
to enter a competition to study at the Conservatory of
Music. The compulsory pieces, particularly the Czerny
studies, made her life difficult, and winter in the house
was a tense time.

In March, Léandre and Gabrielle went with Rose to
the big city for the admission test. They stayed for several
days. During that time, Léandre met those in charge of
the university hospitals and Gabrielle, overcoming her
apprehensions, visited the Holocaust Museum with
Rose. When they came home, they were already, in a
way, elsewhere.

The reply from the Conservatory — Rose was
accepted — arrived at the end of May, at the same time
as the last notebook from Douglas, mailed in New
Guinea. I'm coming back. Wait for me.

Rose awaited her father's return for precisely one hundred days. She was a sorry sight, sleeping only a few hours a night, always dressed in her finest, lunging at the telephone on the first ring and watching out the living room window, lifting the curtain every chance she got.

Meanwhile, they had to clear out the house, which was easier than finding a way to move the tamarack tree. Finally, Gabrielle had an idea.

Rose wept when the tamarack was felled. She watched as it was sawn, barked, and ground. She had trouble letting it go, and was relieved when it came back some weeks later in the form of packages of somewhat rigid sheets. All summer, she listened to Gabrielle typing.

At the end of August, a party put on by their friends and colleagues from the school and the hospital was supposed to be a happy way to mark the departure of the doctor, the teacher, and the young pianist. But Léandre's always clean and carefully folded handkerchiefs wiped more eyes that afternoon than during all the years when they'd been passed from hand to hand in Rivière-aux-Oies.

Early the next morning, Léandre, Gabrielle, and Rose piled into the ramshackle Volvo, with the movers' van close behind them.

Equipped with a false passport, Douglas had trouble covering in the opposite direction the thousands of kilometres that separated him from Rose and Éléna. At twenty-five knots a day, his freighter reached Vancouver in a few weeks. After that, the country turned out to be far more vast than Douglas's savings, as he approached Rivière-aux-Oies on the train. On the platform of the final station he could afford, he decided to go back along the only road on which he was sure to meet only friends. He covered the boreal forest on foot.

When he phoned, the voice was not Gabrielle's, but the lady had not hesitated to give the Patenaudes' new address to Douglas, who was briskly heading there now. He'd had plenty of time to imagine his reunion with Rose. He was prepared for anything, and it hardly mattered to him that his daughter wasn't in Rivière-aux-Oies, as he had hoped. He would go to the village afterwards, to see Éléna again.

The big city was lively, almost beautiful, covered with brand new snow turned rosy by the lazy December sun. In the neighbourhood where Rose lived, the buildings poured their staircases onto the sidewalks. They all looked very much alike and he peered closely at the numbers. When he found the right one, he put off ringing the bell for a moment to smooth himself out and catch his breath. Douglas was happy.

Éléna's hair and her smile opened the door.

Rose didn't greet him by flying into his arms and covering him with kisses as she'd done when she was small. Intimidated, she smiled without saying a word. He took a step towards her to embrace her, but immediately she put between them an object that one second earlier she'd kept hidden behind her back.

"Look, Papa, our tamarack. I have it with me all the time."

It was a book. Around two hundred pages bound between cardboard covers. The title, *The Douglas Notebooks*, went straight to his heart.

The End

Credits

(in order of appearance)

Only once did *Antoine Brady* meet his son Romain. It was in the English part of Kuala Lumpur, where they did not recognize each other in the crowd. Brady was coming out of a grand hotel, satisfied with the discount the Malaysians had agreed to give him on the purchase of some palm oil plantations. The old man still had time to play eighteen holes before he went home. His private airplane crashed into the Pacific Ocean the next night. The billionaire's death was front page news in most Western newspapers two days later.

Alexina Brady got the call announcing the death of her husband just as she was starting to relax at the beautician's. At her request, the receiver was pressed to her ear. Even if she had wanted to ask a question, the white clay mask was already so hard that her mouth couldn't have made a sound. She left the clinic and for ten days devoted herself to arranging a lavish funeral, which she herself attended with her mind elsewhere, at once distracted by the many cameras and knocked out by too much Valium, which she was unable to do without till the end of her life.

Sitting beside her mother in the front row of the cathedral, *May Brady* was poker-faced. The fortune she'd inherited placed her at the head of an empire she had no intention of running but from which she intended to draw the maximum. During the prime minister's eulogy for the dead man, May mentally ran through the Bradys' advisers, asking herself whom she trusted enough to be sure of a rapid and profitable sale of all her shares. A worthy daughter of her father, she sold to the highest bidder before settling permanently in Bermuda.

The priest who had come to close Rose Tavernier's eyes after her husband had beaten her to death often knelt at the end of the last row in the little graveyard of Saint-Lupien. Stricken with remorse after the fire, he insisted on paying out of his own pocket for a new tombstone, and even if no human remains could be buried next to Rose, the names of Éléna and of her father, Eugène, now appeared on the grey marble stone.

In Sainte-Palmyre, *the manor* with its false turrets has been empty since Alexina's death. Very soon, *the music teacher* exiled himself to New York, where he served as a last-minute replacement in a bar on Grove Street. The servants moved away without leaving an address.

The grocer's son to whom Éléna's father had wanted to marry her off died suddenly on the night of the feast of Saint John. Had Éléna married him, she would have been widowed after just a few weeks and would never have known what had become of the big lump of a husband whose body, found in a stream by the police, was hastily buried in a family vault. The name of *Romain Brady* is engraved on a very plain bronze plaque.

The convent of the Little Sisters of Saint Carmel was sold twenty years after Éléna stopped by because of the lack of vocations and because most of the nuns had already moved to the adjacent graveyard. Transformed into a seniors' residence, it offers high-end accommodations that include a restaurant, boutiques, an exercise room, the services of a massage therapist, and a pool. Smokers not welcome.

Not everyone has the means to spend their final days in a former convent. *The trucker* who had renamed Romain Brady grew old alone, far from his family, parked with another thirty-six residents in a building whose common rooms offered a commanding view of the highway. *Madame Taillon*, Éléna's former teacher, as well as *the former chief of Saint-Lupien's police* were no luckier.

As soon as they were able to read and, more important, to calculate, *the inhabitants of Rivière-aux-Oies* seemed more anxious than others to change centuries.

Pike and trout are in short supply in the river, where fishing has become risky, not just on account of access to the water, forbidden in the vicinity of the town, but also because the water itself, less clear than before, gives off a smell that some think is related to the fungicides used to treat the wood in the sawmill. The fries in Rivière-aux-Oies are as greasy and limp as ever, but the tavern that had exclusive rights to them for half a century was shut down and demolished in an hour. There are no more farms on the Back Road, unimaginatively renamed Sixth Street. The wharf has been displaced by a cantilevered bridge that connects the town to its opposite shore, where cement and sheet metal have sprung from the ground. Main Street, which became a boulevard once it had four lanes, can be spotted from a distance thanks to its six-storey hotel and its waterslides. *Gingras the notary* is thrilled. He's making money hand over fist.

After thirteen years in exile, *Douglas Starling* touched down for a while in the big city, where Gabrielle and Léandre had reserved a room for him in their apartment. He stayed there for a few months and still visits, but he preferred to settle in an isolated forest, where he earns his living as a game warden. Even as an old man, he talks affectionately to the tamaracks he runs into, and ever since Rose gave him back his clarinet, he can still, and often does, silence the birds.

Léandre Patenaude has never apologized to Douglas. But he held him so tight, in tears, on the day he met up with him, it was almost as if he had. A conscientious professional, he followed to the letter the Hippocratic Oath until his last day of work at the hospital. He was then seventy years old. Today, he lives surrounded by photos he never tires of looking at, and when he recounts his memories, he always acknowledges that life has been particularly generous to him.

Gabrielle Schmulewitz retired from teaching the year
Rose was admitted to the Conservatory. In the big city,
she gave some thirty speeches a year in the schools.
Before she died, she was able to attend, with Léandre,
the ceremonies commemorating the fiftieth anniversary
of the liberation of Auschwitz. Until the very end, Rose
was her greatest love.

Rose is tall and sensitive like Douglas, vivacious and curly-haired like Éléna, generous and impulsive like Léandre, loyal and indulgent like Gabrielle. She reveres trees to the point of going to the barricades whenever a wooded area is threatened. After the Conservatory, she and some friends established a quartet whose repertoire of nineteenth-century pieces enjoys a certain success. She fell in love with the cellist. They have a son whom they always take with them on tour. His name is Romain.

RECYCLED
Paper made from
recycled material
FSC® C103567